VERTICAL

a novel

WITHDRAWN

Janet Eoff Berend

BREAKAWAY BOOKS
HALCOTTSVILLE, NEW YORK
2013

Vertical
Copyright © 2012 by Janet Eoff Berend

ISBN: 978-1-891369-98-8
Library of Congress Control Number: 2012942678

Published by Breakaway Books
P.O. Box 24
Halcottsville, NY 12438
www.breakawaybooks.com

FIRST EDITION

CONTENTS

ACKNOWLEDGMENTS

I would like to thank the many people who helped make the novel *Vertical* possible. Earliest readers, Clare Zimmerman, Mary Berend, and Corie Heinzelmann, you convinced me I had a story worth telling. Readers Sara Smith, Penny Bernal, Rosie Prine, Kaitlin Wood, Chrissy Teisher, and the book club gals—Brenda, Bridgit, Celine, Marina, Misty and Sally—thanks for the enthusiasm and encouragement. Kerry and Isabella Ojeda, I'm glad that you made me promise not to give up. Ronette Youmans thanks for reading and for helping craft discussion questions. Brendon Anderson and Matt Weiss, I could not have written the skating scenes without you. Thank you for helping me sound legit! My critique group, Vicki Beck and Cynthia Flannery and my fellow writers, Stacey Goldblatt and Sarah Collins Honenberger, thanks for all the help and advice. Garth Battista, a man with true vision, I am forever grateful. Lilly Golden thanks for helping to make the story sparkle and shine. My families, my mom, Linda Casares, my father, Keith Eoff, my sisters Susan Tuminaro and Carolyn Eoff and my nephew and niece in-law, Heath and Brandi Hanchett—all tellers of tall tales. Thanks for loving words as much as I do and for all of the stories that only we think are funny. Bruce and Mary Berend, you have given me nothing but love, care, and support from day one and you always prepare and deliver the most amazing meals. I'm a lucky woman. My kids, Rell and Ben, you and your father are the most important things in my life and you have been nothing but patient and encouraging to a mom obsessed with the need to write. And lastly, to my husband, Jeff, for loving me, for supporting me, for knowing exactly how much half and half to put in my coffee, for reading and editing the manuscript a thousand times. I'm living the dream. Thank you.

To Jeff, Rell, and Ben
with love

1

RAT TRAPS

My mom tells me I have skateboarding on the brain because it's all I ever think about—skateboard wheels clicking across the grooves in pavement, dropping in on the half-pipe—flying, floating . . . totally free. See, for me, the next best thing to actually skateboarding is thinking about it, so I guess my mom *is* right, I do have skateboard brain, or whatever she calls it. The problem is, having a skateboard brain doesn't always help me "live up to my potential" at my local prison otherwise known as school, and not living up to my potential can be a bad thing. Here's why.

First period starts in exactly sixteen minutes. My lunch sits on the counter and even though I'm in ninth grade, my mom still writes my name, JOSH LOWMAN, with a big black marker on my lunch bag like I'm in kindergarten or something. "Live up to your potential!" "School first!"—that's what my folks say. And things like bad grades, wet towels on the bathroom floor, and *being late for school* are all things that can seriously "restrict" my afternoon skate sessions with my best friend Brendon. I look at the clock— first period starts in exactly fourteen minutes. I grab my lunch and my skateboard and bolt out the door.

Valley View High's not too far from my house and most days, if I skate hard and take the shortcut, I get there in plenty of time.

I fly down the main boulevard and pass under the cheese board—that's what we call the giant billboard that towers over our town. There's this huge picture with these two guys smiling, leaning on a car in a driveway, and at the bottom it says: WELCOME TO GREEN VALLEY, CALIFORNIA—WHERE THE BREEZE FLOWS FREELY THROUGH DEEP VALLEYS AND YOUR NEIGHBORS ARE YOUR FRIENDS. Right! This scraggly dog pops out from nowhere sniffing around and he must think the cheese board's pretty cheesy too 'cause he looks up at the picture of those two guys, sniffs one of the poles that holds the thing up, lifts his leg, and takes a leak. I laugh so hard I almost fall off my skateboard.

I carve a turn into the alley, the dog running beside me like he's my new best friend, when a siren screams in the distance and the little dog stops, points his snout toward the sky, and howls. I'm busy checking out my new friend so I don't see the small chunks of broken glass that wedge themselves underneath my skateboard wheels and the next thing I know everything happens in super-fast motion—my board stops but I keep moving, I fly through the air, and splat, I slam across warbly, pockmarked pavement, then skid to a stop.

Splattered against the pavement, I lie there for a second and all I can think about is stupid Mrs. Fudrucker who's gonna mark me late for first period again, then there'll be the detention notice in the mail and my D in algebra and my mom and dad and restriction. I roll over, lying flat on my back, the blue sky and the cheese board floating above me, and I feel like climbing up on that thing with one of my mom's black markers and writing: WELCOME TO GREEN VALLEY, CALIFORNIA—WHERE YOU WIPE OUT IN DEEP ALLEYS AND IT SUCKS! But I know if my parents get squirrelly about a wet towel on the floor, graffiti will definitely send them over the edge.

I sit up, check out the damage—scratched-up palms, bloody elbow—and I know it sounds impossible, but that's when my morning gets even suckier. Grunts and scratching noises emerge from this car parked against a garage. I look over. It's Lenny—this huge hotshot street skater from our neighborhood. He's in Mrs. Thompson's car, leaning across the front seat, digging around like some kind of wild scavenging hyena. He doesn't see me. I think about grabbing my board and getting the heck out of there, but before I can move he hops out of the car and lands with Mrs. Thompson's wallet in his hand. He rifles through it, grabs a couple plastic cards and dollar bills, and slides them into his back pocket. I'm curled up into a frozen ball hoping I'm invisible when Lenny reaches for his skateboard, turns around to bail, and stumbles over me.

"Jeez, what the—" His face hangs over me; his shadow stretches across the alley like some kind of giant.

"I fell," I say.

He looks around real quick, stares at me real hard, his eyes like laser beams cutting into my flesh. "Hey . . . ya know what happens to rats?" he asks. I shake my head. Out of the corner of my eye I see that little dog duck behind a garbage can. "They get their brains squashed in rat traps, that's what happens." Lenny stands there, his nostrils flared, his teeth clenched, and I wish I could be anywhere else but here. He raises his hand over his head and I think he's gonna bring it down across my body like a sledgehammer, but luckily he just flings Mrs. Thompson's empty wallet and it smacks me in the head. He laughs then skates away.

I peel myself off the asphalt, brush all the dirt and stuff off my clothes, when I feel something press against my leg. It's that stray dog, rubbing against me, whimpering. He looks hungry . . . really hungry. I look at my watch; first period starts in five minutes. I know if I don't get on my board right now and skate as fast as I can . . . I'm gonna be late, but then the dog whines and stares up at me with big eyes. I shake my head and sigh, reach into my backpack, tear my bologna sandwich in half, and drop to one knee. "Here, boy," I say. He wolfs it down then licks my face. I hop on my board and skate the rest of the way to school thinking about what I'd write on that billboard if I had the nerve.

2

NOBODY LIKES A RAT

"Pay attention, she's gonna call on you," I hear him whisper. I turn around to see what the heck is going on and I'm staring straight into the face of Edgar Glunk, his giant owl eyes all big and magnified 'cause of the thick black glasses he's been wearing since the third grade, his nose whistling when he breathes, his puny hand wiggling the back of my stupid, plastic green chair. I rub my eyes and look over my shoulder. Erin Campbell, the hottest freshman at our school, shakes her head and smiles.

Welcome to ninth-grade English class at Valley View High— pure torture. The worst part isn't that I sit in front of Edgar Glunk, who everybody in the whole world knows is totally annoying. Or that I have a piece of gravel stuck in my hand from when I fell this morning. Or that the prettiest girl in the world catches me spacing out again. The worst part is, Edgar always manages to wiggle or tap or make that stupid sound by pushing the spit between his two front teeth, right when I'm getting to the raddest part, right when I'm dropping into The Beast—the giant vert ramp shaped like a gnarly capital U. The truth is I've never dropped into the vert ramp all the way without falling, but I've watched myself do it in my own head so many times that I think I actually know how it feels.

I stand on the deck and get ready. My heart's thumping and I feel all jittery and alive. I wipe the snot from my nose with the back of my hand, focus my eyes, clench my jaw. Finally, I stomp on the front of my board, lean forward, and drop in. I race down the first wall, charge up the second, and shoot out the top of the ramp, one arm reaching between my knees, grabbing my board and pressing it to the bottom of my feet, my other arm stretched out like the giant wing of a giant airplane, and I'm flying, weightless, soaring through the sky like a crazy, blazing comet.

And that's when it happens. Edgar Glunk will wiggle my chair or kick my seat or tap his pencil or whisper or sneeze. That's when I realize, of course I'm not dropping into the vert ramp, soaring through the sky like some kind of totally sick skating legend. Of course not! Ya know why? One reason . . . high school.

I'm in deep space right before stupid Edgar Glunk wiggles my chair and my English teacher, Ms. Moreland, calls on me. I'm supposed to be paying attention to her yammering on about some stupid vocabulary word of the day. Lucky for me the word's written on the board with the definition: CATAWAMPUS (ADJECTIVE)— CROOKED, SIDEWAYS. She asks me to make a sentence with it so I come back from space just in time to blurt out the words, "I landed the front-side air catawampus and cracked my head open." The class laughs. Ms. Moreland laughs too. She has a pretty good sense of humor . . . for a teacher.

Finally the last bell of the day rings. When we're finally released from Valley View torture chamber, me and Brendon show up at our usual meeting spot, toss our boards on the pavement, and head for the skate park. Racing across cracks in the sidewalk, our boards make that sweet, clicky sound until we come to an intersection and have to stop at a red light. We stand on the corner and wait to cross. Mrs. Thompson's car cruises by on the back of a tow truck—the window's all smashed in, the door gnarly and dented too. For a second, I start thinking about ol' Mrs. T. When me and Brendon were in sixth grade we needed money so we could buy new wheels for our skateboards and stuff and Mrs. T. paid us to walk her dog and do some yard work. She always paid us extra too.

"Hey, Brendon," I say, "what would you do if you saw someone do something really bad to someone really nice?"

He shrugs. "I dunno."

"Would you tell?"

He shakes his head. "Nobody likes a rat."

The light turns green and we skate off.

We get to the skate park and there's already like twenty kids skating the street course. We pay our three bucks, slap on our pads, and head in.

"Vert ramp's empty. Let's go," I say and toss my backpack under a bench.

Brendon's still fidgeting with his elbow pad trying to get it to fit right. "Vert's lame," he says.

"No it's not."

"Dude, just 'cause you skate the mini ramp doesn't make you a vert skater. You're not legit until you've conquered the beast." He points his finger toward the super-hectic two-story ramp.

"Oh yeah, let me see you drop in, then." I look at him to see if he takes the bait, and he smiles.

I can't believe Brendon's gonna go for it. We cruise past mini land. It's full of little quarter-pipes and other small ramps and stuff and even though it's for beginners I still like to skate there every once in a while. It reminds me of when me and Brendon started out. As we skate by, a bunch of kids stand at the top of a little quarter-pipe. One kid goes for it. He stomps on the front of his board, drops in, and races down the bank. He gets a little wobbly toward the bottom, but he pulls it and all his buddies hoot and holler and cheer for him. Totally cool.

Brendon and me get to the bottom of the vert ramp and climb the stairs to the top. We stand there and look around for a while. You can practically see our whole town from up there, everything, Valley View High, Old Oaks Park, the tops of trees and cars cruising around on the streets below us. Brendon walks over to the edge and so do I. Staring down into the belly of the beast makes my stomach flip.

"You gonna do it?" I ask.

Brendon stands there, staring down, never taking his eyes off the vertical drop. "Nah." He shakes his head. "I'd rather skate the street course."

He turns around, his board dangling from his hand, and bolts down the stairs. I grab my board and follow.

There're all kinds of rails, funboxes, and ledges and stuff in the street course. Skaters fly and launch and fall everywhere—super hectic. Brendon drops his board on the pavement, takes a few pushes, and enters the mayhem. I'm not into skating the street stuff so I head over to the mini ramp and skate until I'm good and sweaty and my legs feel tired and wobbly. I meet back up with Brendon and we head over to the front of the skate park to grab a drink out of our backpacks.

Me and Brendon stand in the shade taking long pulls from our water bottles when I hear his voice. I look toward the entrance. Lenny's standing there. He's at the front of the skate park waiting to come in. I shove my water in my backpack. "Dude, let's bail," I whisper, but Brendon doesn't move. We stand there lurking while Lenny and Skeet, the skate park attendant dude, talk and I'm praying that Lenny doesn't see me.

"You can't skate here without pads and a helmet," Skeet says.

Lenny leans against the counter. "Who are you, the police?"

"Look, the rules are the same as always. They haven't changed and they're not gonna." Skeet points to the giant poster of rules hanging on the wall. "Wear a helmet and pads at all times, put your trash in the trash can, and respect all skaters—those are the rules. If you don't wanna follow 'em go skate the cement bowl at Old Oaks Park. You can do whatever you want there—bust your head open like a watermelon. I don't care."

He's right too; you *can* do whatever you want at Old Oaks. There're no rules and you don't have to pay anything. You're supposed to wear a helmet, but nobody does. Every once in a while the cops cruise by and everyone slaps a helmet on, but as soon as they leave everyone takes them off again.

Lenny turns, takes some money from one of his buddies, and slaps it on the counter. "Here," he says and cruises into the skate park followed by his crew of morons.

I look down at the ground. Lenny skates past and luckily he doesn't see me. I peel off my knee pads one at a time. "Let's get outta here," I say to Brendon.

"You nuts? I'm not done. One more quick sesh," he says and hops on his board and takes off.

Crap. I kick my backpack out of the way, put my pads back

on, and skate after him.

When we get to the street course, Lenny's standing at the top of a ledge hassling some little kid. The poor kid's cheeks are super red and he looks like he's gonna pee his pants. "I'm sorry . . . I didn't mean to," the kid stammers.

Lenny shoves him. "Ever drop in on me again and I'll pummel you, understand? Now get outta here."

The kid pops his board into his hand and I can tell he's trying as hard as he can not to cry. He turns around to leave and Lenny hawks a giant loogy right at him; it lands on his elbow pad and drips down the side. I can't believe it. I look at Brendon and shake my head. "Lenny thinks he's *so* tough, he's never conquered the beast—he's never dropped in vert," I say.

"Doesn't have to. Everybody knows he's top dog around here."

"So he can spit on people and break into—"

"Look, he's older than us and he can out street-skate anyone in town. He can do whatever he wants."

"'Cause he can street-skate? Is that what you think?"

"Well whaddya gonna do about it? Punch him?"

"Somebody's gotta do something. I could tell someone. That's what I could do. I saw him break into Mrs. Thompson's car this morning, steal her money, credit cards, and stuff."

"He ripped off Mrs. T.?"

I turn my head toward the vert ramp. It juts up into blue sky, towering over everything in our skate park, everything in our town. "I tell the police and Lenny could get in a lot of trouble," I say.

"Tell the police and you die. You'd be the biggest rat in Green Valley, California, and nobody'd ever talk to you again."

"He'd go to jail, ya know . . . he'd go away for good."

"Josh . . . *nobody* likes a rat."

I look at the street course. Lenny airs over a set of stairs and his crew of idiots stands around and watches. "Let's get outta here," I say. We pop off our helmets, scoop up our boards, and head for the exit.

FALLING

I hate falling . . . I mean, I'm a skater so falling is a part of the deal, but I still don't like to fall. I know it's not cool to wear a helmet, but I actually don't mind it when I'm skating really gnarly ramps, even though my head gets all sweaty. I figure if I'm gonna fall I like having a little bit of protection—something to help my sponge brain out. I also wear knee pads when I skate the half-pipe. Even though I wear pads, my knees are *super* thrashed. They're all knobby with a bunch of scars and stuff . . . battle scars.

The thing about skating is you have to learn how to fall. The only problem is when you're skating down an alley and there's a bunch of broken glass that you don't see—there's not much you can do about how you fall. But when you're skating a pool or ramp and you're in the air, you kinda know when you're gonna eat it. You can feel it. You'll be up in the air trying to pull a new trick or something and your feet aren't right, or your body's turned funny—catawampus—and you *know* the fall is coming, so you get your knees underneath you, land on your pads, slide down the face of the pool or ramp, and it's all good . . . but still . . . I hate falling.

The one and only time I dropped into the vert ramp I fell. It sucked! You don't even know how bad it sucked. I didn't get my knees underneath me in time, or was going so frickin' fast flying

VERTICAL

down that beast that I took the fall on my side. I could feel my guts bounce around inside of me, and my shoulder felt like someone whaled on me with a sledgehammer. As soon as I hit the ground I heard Brendon yell down from the top, "Dude, are you all right?" I just lay there and put my fist up in the air. I wanted to cry it hurt so bad, but I didn't.

Maybe that's the worst thing about falling when you're a skater, I mean besides the pain—you're not allowed to cry. It's kinda like this rule that everyone follows, but no one ever talks about—skaters don't cry. We kick stuff and throw our boards and cuss and stuff, but no crying. I mean you would be a total wuss if you started bawling and the whole skate park would make fun of you for the rest of your life if they saw even one little tear.

The last time I cried I was a kid. I fell dropping in on the mini ramp, but that's different, I was twelve. The rules are different now. So I didn't cry when I fell on the vert ramp, even though it hurt so bad I could feel my nuts suck in close to my body and I thought I was going to hurl from the pain—I didn't cry. I lay there for a couple minutes, closed my eyes, bit my lower lip, and finally stood up. I hobbled over to the side of the ramp and sat down on my skateboard. I took the rest of the afternoon off, which sucked—a whole afternoon of skating, down the drain. I mean I'll skate the vert ramp from the bottom, pump the walls till I'm nice and high, but dropping in from the top—that's sketchy . . . *super sketchy*.

Brendon says skating vert's lame, not 'cause it's super sketchy or 'cause he's afraid of falling. He just thinks it's boring. He likes street skating 'cause it's always changing and the vert stuff always stays the same. The funny thing is . . . that's exactly why I like vert ramps—you know what you're up against . . . they never change.

19

Me and Brendon are gonna skate our brains out this weekend. Maybe I'll talk him into skating some vert so I can practice. Work on not falling. The thing is, Brendon's mom met some new guy. Her car wouldn't start in the grocery store parking lot and some random guy gave her a jump start. It seems like she's always falling for some new guy, but whatever, it's cool, 'cause every time Brendon's mom gets a new boyfriend, Brendon spends a lot of time at my house, like he's my brother or something. That means we'll hang out, eat burritos, play video games, skate, and hopefully . . . not fall.

EARTHQUAKE DRILLS

Today I'm sitting in English class trying to not die from boredom. I'm flipping my mini finger skateboard onto the spine of my notebook when this stupid alarm goes off. I swear it scares the crap out of me. It's an earthquake drill. So we all get under our desks, which is *totally* lame if you ask me. So there's an earthquake and we're supposed to get under our little desks while the ground is sliding around underneath us? Who do they think we are . . . idiots? I mean come on, if there's ever an earthquake for real, I'm out! I'm not gonna sit there under my desk like some lamo waiting for the roof to cave in.

Anyway, I'm sitting there trying to not let my hair touch any of the dried-up, skanky gum wads that are stuck to the bottom of my desk, which has now become my ceiling, when I hear someone whisper my name. *It's probably Edgar Glunk,* I think to myself, but when I turn my head and see who it is, I get this lump thingy in my throat 'cause it's Erin Campbell.

I'm all balled up under my desk so I scrunch around to face her and she's scrunched up under her desk too. Her long brown hair touches her knees and her shiny lips move but I can't really hear what she's saying. I lean toward her and she smells like bubblegum and vanilla ice cream. Brendon had a crazy crush on her back in eighth grade. He even went out with her for like a week or something. He said he gave her the tongue. Right! Brendon Johnson gave Erin Campbell the tongue. I swear he's so full of it sometimes.

So anyway, there *I* am scrunched up under my desk next to Erin Campbell who is scrunched up under *her* desk and you're never gonna believe this—she asks me for my mini skateboard. I lean over to hand it to her and she smells *soooooo* good. She takes the mini skateboard and holds it in her hand. She checks out the little trucks and wheels and stuff. She asks me how to work the thing, but before I can answer she puts her fingers on the board, pops it, and almost lands a super-sick flip trick on her first try!

"No way, I can't believe you almost pulled that!" I tell her.

"It's the *landing*," she says. And she's totally right. It is the landing. It's *always* the landing.

She hands me back my mini skateboard and then Ms. Moreland tells us to get back in our seats. She goes over the vocabulary word of the day: STOIC (ADJ.)—NOT SHOWING ANYONE HOW YOU FEEL. Then she assigns each one of us in the class our very own copy of some lame book called *The King of the Flies* or something. Perfect. More homework.

MAXIMUM BROTHERHOOD

Finally Saturday comes around and me and Brendon are ready for some hard-core skating. First we head to our old elementary school. We hop the fence and head straight over to the staircase—it has like seven stairs and this heinous handrail—we call it the chum bucket, or the chum, or the bucket. We've been skating there forever. So anyway, we show up at the bucket and start skating.

Brendon goes first. He keeps bailing midair, 'cause he doesn't have enough speed or his feet aren't right, but he doesn't give up, he grabs his board and stomps up to the top of the stairs. He scoots way back and he looks all serious and stuff. Then he takes four or five pushes, gets a lot of nice speed, and races right toward the staircase. He pops the tail, sucks his knees into his chest, and busts this *massive* ollie and he's flying over the stairs, hovering above his skateboard like it's a magic carpet.

While he soars through the air like a maniac, he twists his body around just so and before you know it lands the tail of his board right on the handrail. And it's super rad, 'cause now he's gliding, sliding along that buttery rail, and you can hear the clink, grind, swish sound echo into the hallway of the empty school. His wheels smack the concrete and Brendon lands on his rolling skateboard, perfectly balanced, crouched down like some kind of tiger ready to spring. And he pulls it. You shoulda seen it. It was sooo *sick.* I mean it was *total* triumph. Brendon Johnson flying, gliding, sliding down the handrail, readjusting, balancing, reacting . . . bam—he lands the tailslide.

I stand there with my mouth gaping open and Brendon smiles and pumps his fist in the air. Then I hoot and holler and Brendon starts doing the same and we dance around the chum bucket like two little kids who just hit the jackpot at Chuck E. Cheese's. Then it's my turn.

I can't land anything at first and then, finally, something magical happens, like the skate gods are smiling down on us or something. I race toward the stairs with lots of speed and right before I launch over them, I snap the tail, slide my front foot forward, and flick the nose of my board. Pulling my knees to my chest, I watch my board spin below me. I float over the stairs, catch the board grip-side up with my feet like I have magnets in the bottoms of my shoes, and kerplunk onto the pavement, two feet solid on the deck of my board. I *land* it and I'm not even a really good street skater. Me and Brendon . . . we can't believe it. We just keep skating and skating and skating. We fall sometimes, but we keep landing tricks too. It's the most *epic* skate session!

We'd skate at the chum bucket till dark if we could, but we get so frickin' hungry our legs start to wobble and we're thirsty and sweaty and tired. So we skate over to Federico's #3 Taco Shop. We sit there and attack our food like a couple of starving animals, and for some reason I start thinking about school and how I'm so glad I'm not there right now.

"Dude, I sit next to your ex-girlfriend in my English class," I say between giant mouthfuls of burrito.

"Which one?"

"Right, Brendon, like you have a million girls or something, you know which one—your old girlfriend, old flame, ex-lover." I take a giant swig of soda and let out a massive burp. "Erin Campbell."

He stops eating for like three seconds and looks up. "Dude, *no way!*"

"Yep—sit right next to her in English."

"Holy crap—Erin Campbell . . . she's *so* hot," he says. He shakes his head, takes a long pull of soda, and keeps mauling his food.

I put my scraps on my plate and push it to the center of the table. Brendon reaches over, grabs the burrito nub from my plate, and inhales that too, and when he's finally done eating he starts carving his initials into the table with his little Swiss Army knife. We sit there for a while—no talking, just me and Brendon, sitting in the orange booth, taking it all in, and just when we're nice and relaxed we hear the door open and who walks in but stupid butthead Lenny and his crew of morons. As soon as he sees us, he walks over to our table and stares at me for a long time.

"Look who's here, two overbaked, crusty pieces of dog crap," he says. And of course his crew of idiots laugh like they never heard anything funnier in their lives. He looks right at me.

"Hey, Lowlife, give me couple dollars."

I don't look up from the orange table. "I don't have two—"

"I said give me some money now, I'm starving." He starts leaning over my way like he is gonna grab me, turn me upside down, and empty my pockets, but before he can get his grimy, fat hands on me, Brendon reaches into his pocket and slaps two dollar bills on the table.

"Take it," he says and flicks the money toward him.

Lenny stands there for a second . . . he scoops up the bills and puts them in his pocket. "Later, wusses," he says, and they all walk away laughing.

It's quiet for a second. Me and Brendon sit there staring at the table in front of us, then Brendon looks at me. "It's just two stupid dollars," he says.

"Lenny's a jerk."

"Whatever."

We stand up and grab our boards 'cause there's no way we're gonna sit there in Federico's with those bottom feeders so we bail. We think about going over and skating the bowl at Old Oaks Park since we know that Lenny and his morons aren't there, but we don't want to risk ruining the best day of our lives with a crappy session. So we skate over to the Thrifty Save Drugstore instead. Brendon walks straight to the toy aisle and starts looking around. He grabs some black-box-looking thing, then looks over his shoulder to make sure nobody's watching and opens the package. He grabs some batteries off the shelf and opens that package too.

"What the heck ya doing?" I ask.

"Putting batteries in this fart machine." He looks up and grins.

He walks over to an empty aisle, plants the little black speaker thing behind some cough drops, cruises to the end of the aisle, and ducks behind a rack of T-shirts. I follow him and we crouch down, hiding . . . waiting. Finally a man walks down the aisle. He stops in front of the cough syrup, picks up a bottle, and reads the label. Brendon has the little remote thing in his hand. He presses the button and an enormous fart blasts through the entire store. The man looks around like he's just committed the biggest crime in the universe or something. He sets down the bottle of cough syrup, does a U-turn, and scurries away.

Brendon and me pop out from our hiding spot and we explode. We're out-of-control laughing, *really* hard and *really* loud. Brendon's face gets super red, like a piece of Hot Tamales candy or something, and I have tears in my eyes and my sides hurt even from laughing so hard. I'm surprised some grumpy old lady in a red Thrifty Save employee's vest doesn't come over and kick us out, but luckily nobody bothers us. We stay there for a while, waiting for our next victim, but it's slow and nobody comes by. We get tired of waiting so we bail our special-ops undercover fart mission and head over to the magazine aisle instead.

I'm sitting on my skateboard reading a skateboard magazine when I hear soft footsteps heading my way. I scooch over to the side of the aisle to let the person get by and when I look up Mrs. Thompson is standing there. I try and bury my head in my magazine, but it's too late, she recognizes me.

"Well, hello, Josh . . . Brendon," she says. "How are you boys?"

"Fine, thanks. And you?" I say.

"I'm okay—you know . . . getting along. You boys come see me when you need to earn some extra money now, you hear?" She smiles and shuffles down the aisle to the cash register.

I think she might think we're still in sixth grade, but whatever. I flip to the center of my skate magazine. A skater airs over a set of eight stairs. I flip through a few more pages, but I can't really concentrate 'cause I start thinking about Mrs. Thompson, her broken window, her missing credit cards, that stupid loogy dripping off that kid's elbow, Lenny and the two dollars from Federico's that aren't his.

"Hey, Brendon," I say, "I know nobody likes a rat, but somebody's gotta do something about Lenny."

"Not this again."

"He's a total jerk."

"There's nothin' you can do about it."

"I'm gonna tell my parents that he stole from Mrs. Thompson and stuff. See if they can help."

"Don't do it."

"Why not?"

Brendon flips through a few pages of his magazine then looks up. "'Cause you're gonna get murdered, that's why, and everyone's gonna know you're a snitch and I'm your best friend, so they're gonna think I'm a snitch and the whole town's gonna be against us."

"But Lenny—he's . . . somebody's gotta do something."

Brendon stares at his magazine, but I can tell he's not really reading it or anything. "Do it and I'll never talk to you again," he says. He stands up and shoves his magazine back on the rack.

I think he's joking, just messing around, but when I look at his face he's serious . . . totally serious. I can't believe it. *He can't do that. He can't just quit talking to me, we're practically brothers.* He scoops up his skateboard and cruises over to the candy aisle.

We both stand there and look at all the different kinds of candy for a while. I grab a bright blue bottle of Maximum Sugar Blast and hold it in my hand. Brendon used to be totally addicted to Maximum Sugar Blast when we were in the fifth grade. I stare at the bright blue bottle and that's when it comes to me.

"Hey, ya know that skate company we're gonna own someday?" I say.

"Yeah."

"Let's call it 'Maximum Brotherhood.'"

Brendon looks at me and nods. "Okay."

6

ONE—TWO PUNCH

In some ways I think high school is the biggest, gnarliest beast of them all. I mean, does anyone realize how totally extremely lame this whole "go to high school, go to college, get a job" thing is? It all starts with high school and it's evil, like a gateway drug. I mean, my big sister had her face in a book the whole time she was in high school. Now she's in college and guess what? She has her face in a book like twenty-four hours a day. And when I ask her why, she tells me so she can get a good job and stuff. So she's had her face in a book since forever and then she's gonna get a job and have no life 'cause she's gonna have to work her butt off there too. Doesn't that sound just wonderful . . . fantastic! It makes me want to puke just thinking about it.

So you go to high school, you get into college, you get a job, just like your parents and teachers and everyone else says you should, and now you have a job and make money and stuff, but when do you have time to skate? You don't. You don't skate. You don't drop in. So you play by the rules, but you still get totally burned. What's the point? What's it matter if you have some job, but you're totally miserable? And where does the nasty beast start gnawing on your leg, sucking the life out of ya? . . . High school!

I'm not the only one who thinks high school is 100 percent totally lame, believe me. High school really ticks Brendon off too 'cause in junior high he didn't have to try at *all* and he would still pull good enough grades. He never *ever* did homework, but he would always pull good grades on tests, so he would always pass *no* problem. Boy, those days are over. The only class Brendon is passing is gym. Today after school, the vice principal, Mr. Bedcraft, aka Mr. Buttcrack, called Brendon into his office. I can totally picture it. Brendon sits there squirming around in his chair. Buttcrack leans an elbow on his big ol' desk, his nose hairs shimmying around when he breathes. He's being all serious and I know Brendon—all he's thinking about is the sick tailslide he pulled at the skate park yesterday afternoon.

But seriously, Buttcrack did call Brendon into his office and tell him that if he "didn't get his act together by the end of the semester, he would be in jeopardy of not graduating from high school on time." Whatever. Like Brendon cares. The thing is, Brendon's mom, she's busy meeting random guys in parking lots who give her battery a jump start, so she's not paying attention, and Brendon—he's totally free. He's lucky. He can do anything he wants. He gets to skate and play video games and watch TV until midnight if he wants. Total freedom. I swear, he's got it so good, sometimes I wish my parents didn't "care" so much.

Brendon wastes so much time getting hassled by the vice principal that we don't have time to go to the skate park. We skate in front of my house on these grind rails we built in metal shop when we were in eighth grade instead. I'm having a crappy session. I can't land *anything,* so I just sit on the curb and watch Brendon skate. A car cruises down the street. Brendon stops skating long enough to let it pass and we're pretty sure it's Vice Principal Buttcrack.

Brendon waits for the car to get like a block away and then he marches into the middle of the street and flips him the bird. Brendon stands in the street for like thirty seconds with his finger raised in the air likes he's the Statue of Liberty or something, but Buttcrack had already turned the corner, so I don't think he saw it. Brendon stands there peering down the street, then he comes and sits on the curb next to me. He pulls a sweet little skate tool out of his back pocket and starts messing around with the trucks on his board.

"So what happens if you flunk all your classes?" I ask.

"Nothin'." Brendon keeps turning the wrench, tugging on his trucks to see if they wiggle.

"But did he say you'd have to leave school—like go somewhere else or something?"

"Probably."

"Maybe we should start studying together . . . maybe I could help you."

Brendon stops fiddling with his trucks and looks at me. "*You're* gonna help *me*? You serious?"

"I'm just saying . . . we could do some homework every once in while, that's all."

"I hate homework . . . waste of time." He stands up, grabs his board, and starts skating again—busting ollies and tailsliding along the buttery rail. And that's the thing about Brendon . . . all he really cares about is skating.

We get done messing around in the street and I ask my mom if Brendon can eat dinner with us. Of course she says yes. So there we are sitting at the dinner table—my mom, dad, Brendon, my little brother, Mikey, and me, and we aren't there for more than five minutes when my mom and dad start hassling me.

"Josh, your progress report came in the mail today," my mom says. Oh crap, I know this isn't going to be good.

"You know the rules in this house," my dad pipes in.

"Yeah, you know the rules, Joshey, there's rules in this house," Mikey sings out. I feel like picking up a piece of garlic bread and hucking it at him from across the table, but of course I don't 'cause he's in first grade and that's one of the rules, no roughing up my annoying little brother—my parents totally freak if I even finger-flick him in the ear every once in a while. My mom keeps at it.

"You have a D-minus in algebra and if you don't do something soon, you're going to fail."

Brendon stares down at his plate of spaghetti and keeps eating, but I feel him kick me under the table. I look over. He has this goofy, smart-aleck grin smeared across his face. What a butthead! He's flunking out and I have one stupid D-minus and my parents are freaking out—they're like, *almost failing a class, ahhhhh, Armageddon, the world is ending!*

My dad's the one who delivers the one–two punch. I have to come straight home right after school, finish all my homework, no skateboarding for *two weeks. And* I have to go to math tutoring at Bright Horizons Learning Center. Total torture! I sit there for the rest of dinner. All I hear is forks scraping plates and Mikey slurping spaghetti, but I don't feel like eating anymore. I've completely lost my appetite.

7

BRIGHT HORIZONS

So my parents make me go to this tutoring place for math. They tell me I have to "think about my future" and that "the decisions that I make right now can have an impact on the rest of my life." You know, the usual crap you hear from grown-ups, especially stressed-out parents. All I know is, I should be out skating with Brendon, but instead I'm sitting in the front seat of my mom's mini van going to some lame tutoring place. To make it even worse we drive by Old Oaks Park and I can see skaters airing out of the bowl as we pass. And then my mother starts in.

"You know, I can't even take your little brother to this park in the afternoons anymore. The skateboarders have taken it over,"

Here we go. I look down at my feet. "They're just skating, Mom—that's all they want to do."

"I don't have a problem with them because they're skating, Josh. I just don't like that they leave their trash everywhere and they cuss all the time; even when little kids are standing right next to them, they cuss. They have no respect . . . they're like a pack of wild animals."

"It's not *that* bad."

"It is that bad. You'll see. Those boys are out of control, and the neighbors around here aren't happy. Before you know it the city's going to fill that concrete skate bowl full of dirt and make a giant flower garden out of it and I'll be happy when they do."

Seriously . . . my mom's *freaking out* because some skaters want to be free for like *five minutes* of their lives. She's stressing out about *nothing* like *all* adults do and I can't hang out and skate with Brendon. I keep my mouth shut 'cause if I say anything else she'll keep going on and on and on and I'm really not in the mood.

So I go into this Bright Horizons place and I can tell right away it's going to be super lame. There's all of these dumb posters on the wall that are supposed to "inspire" you to do good in school or something. There's this one poster with these guys riding their bikes up some big hill and it has this fancy word, PERSEVERANCE, in big red letters down at the bottom. Whatever. So they make me take all of these annoying tests to see what I know about math and I want to tell them if I knew anything about math I wouldn't be here! So of course the tests come back and they tell me I don't know very much about algebra. How lame is that? So they tell my mom I'm going to need tutoring twice a week until the end of the school year. I feel like crawling under the table and dying right there.

They send me over to the "math lab" to meet my tutor. I'm thinking he's going to be some nerd with a pocket on his shirt and pants above his ankle and a piece of tape holding his glasses together, just like the way nerds look on all those old TV shows, but this guy comes over and introduces himself and he doesn't look nerdy at all. His name is Zander and he's a college student or something. He shakes my hand, tells me we're going to be working together, and tells me to bring my math homework with me to our next session. And then we leave, thank God!

I'm starting to be in a better mood 'cause I beg and plead with my mom and even though I'm on restriction she agrees to let me skate in front of our house before dinner. On our way back home we drive by Old Oaks Park again. I look over and see a bunch of skaters. I recognize stupid Lenny sitting on the wall of the bowl. He has a cigarette hanging out of his mouth and he's sitting next to someone, and as we get closer I recognize the person sitting on the wall next to him—it's Brendon. He's sitting next to Lenny and they're laughing at something, like they're the best friends in the whole world.

"What's the matter, Josh?" my mom ask from off in the distance.

"Nothing," I mutter, and for some reason I don't really feel like skating anymore.

8

WORD OF THE DAY

I feel like a robot death zombie now that I'm on restriction. All I do is go to school and do homework, and my teachers try their hardest to fill my brain with useless crap. We have to do the weirdest things while we're in school sometimes. Like in science class. Mr. Nash walks into the room carrying this huge stack of paper plates and tells us we're gonna do this "really cool lab" and he's super excited like it's the sickest thing in the world or something. So he stands in the front of the class, cuts one of the paper plates in half, holds the two halves of the plates together, and starts sliding them up and down. Very serious and very dramatic like, he asks the class, "Do you know what this is?" We all look at each other and I'm waiting for someone to yell, *Yeah it's the paper plate you just cut in half, you moron,* but of course nobody does. Mr. Nash, pauses for a second, looks down at the ground, then up, and then he whispers full of drama, "It's an earthquake."

He talks forever about fault lines and tremors and the ground shifting. He says that we're all sitting on these giant tectonic earth plates or something. I kind of remember studying this stuff in elementary school. The thing is, no one knows when the plates are gonna move, when the ground's gonna shift right under our feet and change everything. I guess that's why they make us do those stupid earthquake drills where we sit under our desks and wait for the world to end.

Anyway, Mr. Nash makes us do this lab where we cut paper plates in half and slide one side up and the other side down. Each time we move the plate a little we have to record "the magnitude of the earth's movements." That's what we do the rest of the class.

But in English class something kind of interesting happens. The word of the day is ANOMALY. It means "an exception to a rule," which is impossible to understand so Ms. Moreland explains that it's when something is different from how it's supposed to be. The interesting part is that Ms. M. calls on Erin Campbell to use the word in a sentence and do you know what she says? She says, "Josh is an anomaly because he's a guy *and* he's nice." The rest of the class lets out this giant "Ohhhhhhhhh," like she's in love with me or something, but I'm pretty sure she doesn't mean it that way. I'm not exactly sure what she means, but I think maybe she's saying that for her, the rule is that guys are mean, but not me, so see, I'm the exception. I'm not sure, but I think maybe it's a compliment.

Then Ms. Moreland starts talking about this book we're reading, *The Lord of the Flies.* It's this kind of okay story about a bunch of boys who get lost on this island and they kind of start to go wild, but in a bad way. She talks for a *long* time. She keeps going on and on about symbols or something like that and how writers say one thing but really mean another, which is *totally* lame if you ask me.

I pay attention for like five minutes but then it gets all warm in her classroom and stuff and I feel all woozy and tired, so I pull my hoodie way down over my head and I kind of take a little nap but with my eyes half open. I snap out of it when she writes a question on the board. She says that we're supposed to figure out the meaning of this big shell that those lost boys find on their island and now, I'm just like one of those boys from the story—*I'm totally lost!*

Luckily, Ms. M. tells us to find a partner and talk about the question before we write up our answer. I'm sitting closest to Erin so I scooch my desk next to hers and we start talking. I ask her what she thinks that stupid shell from the story stands for because I have no idea and I need someone to tell me so that I can do Ms. Moreland's dumb assignment and not get in even more trouble with my mom and dad. But Erin doesn't talk about shells or lost boys really, and of course we have to kind of keep our voices low and look like we're talking about Ms. Moreland's assignment or we'll get busted.

"Do you still hang out with Brendon?" she asks.

"Yep, every day."

"I was in algebra with him last year. He's a total math genius."

"That loser? I wish he was smarter," I whisper back.

"What are you talking about? He *is* smart."

"Yeah, except the jackass is flunking every class except gym. He's gonna get kicked out of here if he doesn't get it together soon and I'm gonna be left here . . . alone."

She shakes her head. "Skaters . . . they *all* drop out, even the smart ones . . . like they're a lost cause or something."

"Lost cause . . . Think *Brendon's* a lost cause?"

"I don't know." She shrugs.

I look out the window. A group of football players passes by our classroom, pushing each other and laughing. "You should call him sometime," I say.

She smiles. "Maybe I will."

But I know she won't. I mean, I don't think she'll really call Brendon. She always sits at the lunch tables where all the jocks hang out. There's this one guy, Danny Ramsey. He's this big senior dude, this super-jock guy. He's like the king of the school or something and Erin always sits at his lunch table.

"Maybe you really could call Brendon sometime, ya know? Like, for real. You could help him study and stuff. Maybe he'd listen to you and then he wouldn't be lost and he wouldn't get kicked out of here and leave me stranded. He's such a loser sometimes, I swear." She laughs a little bit, stares out the window, twirls her hair. I glance at my empty sheet of paper but I don't know what to write so I just sit there and chew on the end of my pencil.

She turns to me. "I *could* call him," she says, ". . . but you know what everyone would say around here, don't you? They'd say he's my boyfriend and it'll turn into this *huge* scandal, and the gossip hounds will all go crazy."

I look at her with a blank stare. "The what?" I say.

"The gossip hounds . . ."

"Whaddya talkin' about?"

"That's what I call them—*you know* . . . the gossip hounds . . . like all of the totally mean moldy girls at this school, who fight over all of the dumb moldy guys who aren't even nice to them, and they spread all of these rumors that aren't even true . . . I wish they'd just leave people alone."

"Gossip hounds," I say.

"It's like they bite me *all* the time."

"They *bite* you?"

"Well, no not *really*, they just talk about me . . . make up a bunch of stuff that isn't true. You know who Danny is, right . . .

Danny Ramsey?" I nod. Of course I know who Danny Ramsey is. Everyone knows who Danny Ramsey is.

"Well, me and Danny . . . we've known each other since I was like two. My mom and his mom are best friends, so Danny . . . he's practically like my big brother or something and sometimes I hang out with him and his friends, and *all* the little gossip hounds around here . . . it drives them *crazy*. They make a *big* deal out of it—turn it into something it's not . . . jealous I guess."

"So they come after you with their dumb rumors."

"Exactly—gossip hounds, they're *totally sucky."*

I doodle around on the empty sheet of paper in front of me and we're both quiet for a second. "I think they're more like gossip Chihuahuas," I say.

And she laughs and so do I, 'cause can't you see it? I mean, can't you picture it in your head? There's Erin and Danny, and *all* they're doing is sittin' around the lunch table talking and all of these stupid little Chihuahuas dressed up in those pink ballerina tutu thingies yap and make a fuss and nip at their feet. Those stupid gossip hounds, they're so lame that they're funny.

"Don't worry about the gossip hounds," I tell her. "Everybody knows that none of the stuff they say is true. They're just super lame, that's all." I sit there and tap my pencil against the desk, thinking. She looks down at her paper for a second and then she looks at me and smiles.

"Well . . . I guess you *are* kind of an anomaly then, aren't you?" I tilt my head and look at her kinda funny 'cause I have no idea what she's talking about.

"I mean . . . you're a guy and you're nice and you're even pretty cool," she says, and this time I know for sure that Erin Campbell just gave me a totally legit compliment. Even though we don't get one word written about the stupid English assignment that Ms. Moreland gives us, I don't care 'cause talking to Erin is way better than doing stupid schoolwork.

The bell rings and I rush out to find Brendon at our meeting spot. We eat our lunch and I tell him about English class. I tell him that maybe Erin will call him and that people will think they're boyfriend and girlfriend and it'll drive the gossip hounds crazy and stuff like that. Of course he plays it all casual and cool, like he's some kind of player or something, but I can tell that he's super interested because he wants to know every little word that she said about him. He *totally* flips when I tell him the part she said about skaters, though—that they flunk out of school and all. He says, "Why'd ya tell her I'm flunking? You're such a pile!" Stuff like that. Whatever. It'd be cool if Brendon would at least try. I mean, he could be Erin's anomaly too, right? I mean, why not? He could be a skater and at least pass a few of his classes. Not that he would ever be some kind of school boy or something, but maybe he could at least bring paper and a pencil to class. I swear, he's such a steamy pile of dog crap sometimes.

The next day I walk into English class and I practically have a heart attack. I was so busy doing stuff for my other classes that I completely forgot to do the homework for Ms. Moreland's class, so now I'm ruined because if I don't have all B's and C's by the semester, I'll be on restriction for the rest of my life. Of course I play it all cool, I'm all stoic and stuff, but I feel like screaming or punching something and then, I hear someone whisper, "Hey, Josh . . . take this."

I look over and Erin hands me a piece of paper. It's all typed and neat looking and it has my name in the right-hand corner. It's the answer to the question Ms. Moreland put on the board yesterday and it's like *a page long*. It sounds super smart too. Erin wrote that the shell from the story is some kind of symbol . . . a symbol of order, or something like that, 'cause it keeps things together, like when the lost boys use it in their meetings to make plans on how they're gonna survive and stuff. That stupid shell keeps them together, but when it gets crushed, everything falls apart and those lost boys . . . they go totally wild. And the whole time I thought it was just a shell. Erin . . . she's so smart . . . she makes it seem like it means something else altogether. Anyway, she saves my life by handing me that essay with my name on it and I'm so happy to have something to turn in, I feel like hugging her, kissing her, telling her that she's an anomaly too 'cause she's a girl, she's pretty, she's smart, *and* she's cool . . . but of course . . . I don't.

9

DIFFERENT DIRECTIONS

I finally get off restriction. I think if it would've gone on for even one more day I would have curled up into a ball and died. I see Brendon at lunch and show him this logo I've been working on for our skate company. It's a burrito with these two big eyeballs and the burrito has wings and it's standing on a skateboard and stuff. It sounds weird, but it's actually kind of cool. Even Brendon thinks it's sick. We agree to meet after school and go for a skate session at the skate park. Before lunch is over, Brendon acts all casual and cool and tells me that he talked to Erin. I start messing with him. I punch him and push him. He gets me all stumped over in a half nelson move and starts whaling on me but not too painful or anything. We're just playing around, and then Buttcrack comes over and tells us to knock it off before someone gets hurt. Whatever. School won't even let you have a little bit of fun.

As soon as school gets out, me and Brendon head over to the skate park. We stand in line with all the other skaters, pay our three dollars, put our pads on, and start skating, and even though it's only been a couple weeks since I've skated I feel like an old man, but I don't even care 'cause that cool clickity sound of skate wheels hitting wood ramps makes me feel good. We decide to skate the street course stuff first. Brendon tells me he skated every day while

I was on restriction and that he even bailed his last-period class a couple times to get more skating in. And I can tell he's been skating a bunch too. He keeps trying this one trick over and over. After a while, I get bored with the street stuff so I head for the small half-pipe.

I'm rusty at first. I drop in and do a few rock to fakies just to get warmed up and then I start to feel it. I set up at the top of the mini half pipe. I stomp the front of my board, lean forward, race down the first wall, down into the curved bottom of the ramp, up the other side, and launch into the air. I bend my legs up, reach my hand down between my knees, and indy grab my board, pressing it to the bottom of my feet. I'm in the air now, floating, sailing, flying. I'm up there for a few seconds before I land back in the half-pipe, speed down the wall I just landed on, back through the bottom of the ramp and up to the top of the other side again, and I have speed—lots of speed, but no air this time. Instead I carve a slight turn at the very top of the ramp and pop my front and back trucks onto the coping, and then there's that sound—that sweet sound of trucks grinding metal.

My weight is centered over my board and I float across the coping, 50–50 along the round metal bar, and I feel like I'm moving in slow motion, but I'm not. I'm still moving fast enough to roll back into the ramp and pop out on the other side, and that's all I do for like an hour. I drop in, pull indys and 50–50s, and I'm smiling the whole time—one of those big, grinning, ear-to-ear smiles because you know why? When I hear the sound of wheels rolling on skate ramps and metal trucks grinding coping, when I'm skating . . . I feel free. I'm *so* happy to be skating again I even head over to the vert ramp. It's not too crowded so I start from the bottom and start pumping till I'm over halfway up the sides. I get pretty close to the top, but I bail before I get any higher and I'm stoked 'cause I think that's the highest I've ever gotten up the walls of the beast.

I head back over to the street course to see what Brendon's doing. He's still working on the same trick. I sit on my board and watch him skate. He goes for it a couple more times and almost lands it, but keeps losing his balance. He cusses at his board, super frustrated, but he doesn't give up. Finally he takes a bunch of pushes, ollies, lands the tail on the ledge of the funbox, and slides along the edge. While he's moving, he slides his front foot over to the side of his board, flicks his toe, and pulls his knees up toward his chest all at the same time. Push, flick, pull—just like that, and his board spins underneath him.

He's flying over his spinning board in the air, his arms stretched out like giant wings, his knees bent up toward his chest. He looks down at his board, totally serious, totally focused. His board spins a perfect 360 degrees and floats grip-side up just underneath his feet, and I'm thinking *He's gonna pull it this time, he's gonna land it.* And he does. His board smacks down on the pavement and his feet land perfect, right over both trucks, right on top of his board, and he keeps rolling. I hear him let out a giant whoop and he skates over to me with a giant smile on his face.

"Dude, did you see that?" he says. And of course I tell him how sick it was, that it coulda been a picture in a magazine or something. I stand up and hop on my board. We skate over to our backpacks, pop off our helmets, and take long pulls of water. Our hair is all sweaty and stuck to our heads and stuff. We stand there and the fresh air against our sweaty faces and the cold water sliding down our throats is epic. I look at my watch.

"Dude, I gotta bail . . . math tutoring," I say.

"That's moldy," he says. He takes the last swig of water and tosses the empty bottle toward the green barrel trash can. He looks at me. "Dude . . . your parents are hectic . . . why don't they just leave you alone?"

I shrug. "I don't know . . . they're parents."

"It's like they have you trapped in a cage or something."

"Whatever, I just gotta go to math tutoring, that's all." I peel off my sweaty pads and put them in my backpack. Brendon takes his pads off too. "Whaddya doing? Park's still open a whole 'nother hour," I say.

"I know . . . I'm over this place. Gonna go to Old Oaks . . . skate some more . . . hang out." He pulls at a string that's unraveling on one of his knee pads. I take another drink of water and look down at my shoes.

"You gonna hang out with Lenny?" I ask.

"If he's there. Ya know . . . he's not as bad as you think."

Yeah, right. He's a frickin' caveman. "Whatever," I say.

I take the last swig of my water. We throw our backpacks on and walk out of the skate park together. When we get to the street we hop on our boards. "Later," I say and we skate off—me in one direction and Brendon in another.

10

RESTORATION OF BROKEN PARTS

Zander, my math tutor, is crazy. Not mental, but like kinda cool crazy. So I go to tutoring on Tuesday after skating with Brendon and we work on my math homework. I tell Zander how stupid algebra is, that I'll never use it in my life and I don't understand why I have to learn it in the first place. He nods and we keep working through the problems on my math homework, but before I leave, he tells me to bring one of my old skateboards with me to our next tutoring session. So I do.

I show up on Thursday with one of my old, thrashed skateboards. Zander walks into the math lab carrying a skate tool and tells me to take all the wheels off the trucks. When I have all four wheels stacked in a tower in front of me, he hands me a screwdriver and a wrench and tells me to take the trucks off too. I'm not really sure what any of this has to do with algebra or math tutoring or bright horizons, but I play along anyway. When I have the whole skateboard taken apart he asks me if I can ride it that way, which is a *totally dumb* question because obviously the answer is no, *duh*! Then he asks me why not? Another *dumb* question—because it doesn't have any wheels. And he says that's right, it's broken the way it is, and if I want to ride my skateboard I have to put the broken pieces back together. He says that's what algebra is . . . that if I looked up the definition in the dictionary, it would say "the restoration of broken parts." He tells me before I can put my skateboard back together I have to make some choices.

"Are you gonna put the wheels back on the trucks first and then put the trucks back on the board, or are you gonna put the trucks on first and then put the wheels on the trucks?" he asks. Another dumb question. I tell him I have to do it the second way he said 'cause if I don't, the wheels on the trucks won't give me enough room to fasten the trucks onto the board and I'll be all messed up and I'll have to start over. And he says, "Exactly! You just did algebra!"

I have no idea what he's talking about and Zander can tell that I think he's lost his marbles or something. So he takes the wrench and screwdriver and starts putting the board back together and he talks the whole time. He says all algebra is, is putting things together. He says that anytime you fix something that's broken, you're using algebra because what algebra really is, is a way of thinking. And then he asks me if I know what idea in algebra I used when I had to put my board back together. And of course I shake my head no. He tells me I used "the order of operations" 'cause I had to "perform an operation" on my board and I had to think about what I needed to do first and second to make the "operation" come out good. He says anytime I put one of my skateboards together, I don't even have to think about it—I always know that the trucks go on first. He says it's like an unwritten rule that all skaters know—you always put the trucks on first, and if you don't follow the rule, you'll get all messed up. He says algebra is the same way. There's an order of operations that says what to do first and second, and if we don't do it in the exact order, we'll get all messed up and have to start over, just like when we put a skateboard together.

I sit at the table and doodle on the corner of a piece of paper. "Hey, Zander," I say, "do you think the order of operations works on people?" This time he looks at me like I've lost my marbles. "I mean, if you use the order of operations, if you do everything just right, think you could stop somebody from doing something stupid?"

He looks at me and shrugs. Then I take out my homework and start doing some math problems while Zander finishes putting the wheels back on the trucks. I make sure I do everything in the exact right order, just like Zander says, and I get almost every problem right. Zander hands me my skateboard before I leave and we walk out to the lobby. "Remember, stick to the order of operations and you'll be fine," he says. He turns around and walks away. I notice the back of his T-shirt. "Hey, Zander," I say "Do you skate?" He looks back at me, smiles, and heads back into the math lab. I told you he's crazy.

11

ANTIGONE

In English class we start a new unit on some weird book written like a thousand years ago, by some old guy in a toga. It's called *Antigony* or something. So before we start reading, Ms. Moreland makes us write in our journals. She asks us to write about whether we would risk our lives to stand up for something we believe in. And you know what? I don't think I would, I mean it's your life and if you were dead you couldn't skate, and most of the time if you just stay really low-key and stuff you can pretty much tell people what they want to hear and then do what you want. Like always, Ms. Moreland has us talk about what we wrote with a partner, and of course, I pick Erin and Erin picks me. The thing is, it's a really hard question to answer. So we talk about something different altogether. She tells me she's been talking to Brendon and I practically fall out of my seat. She says they've just been talking to each other a little bit, that she likes talking. So we talk.

I know this sounds funny but she tells me that she feels like we're all standing on one of those giant earth plates that Mr. Nash is always talking about, and it's moving around underneath us and there's nothing we can do about it. And that sounds weird and random and stuff, but I totally understand what she's saying. I mean . . . I think that's what's happening to me and Brendon sometimes, I think those earth plates are moving around underneath us, and I tell Erin that. I can't really explain it or anything, but those earth plates are moving and I know I must sound crazy and stuff, but you know what? She doesn't laugh at me or anything, she just nods and says she completely understands.

Ms. Moreland is kind of moving toward our desks so we have to look busy and stuff, like we're actually talking about English. She saunters over and stands right next to us, so I ask Erin about the question we're supposed to be talking about—I ask her if she would risk her life to stand up for what she believes in. Ms. Moreland is satisfied that we're actually doing our work. She smiles, and moves on to her next prey, and even though Ms. M. is off our backs and we could talk about anything we want, Erin answers the question. You know what she says? She says she *would* risk her life if it would save somebody she loves. I believe her too. I think she would. Erin's tough. Too bad she isn't a skater. Then everyone in the class starts cramming their books and papers into their backpacks. The bell rings. Me and Erin and everyone else in the class stand up, grab our stuff, and stampede out the door.

The next day in English we start that stupid *Antigone* story. Our teacher tells us what it's about so we won't get lost when we're *reading* it, but I get lost when she's *explaining* it 'cause it's such a whacked-out story. Okay . . . so it's about these two brothers who wind up fighting each other 'cause they both want to be king and guess what? The brothers wind up *killing* each other, so none of them gets to be king 'cause they're dead. So their uncle becomes the king instead and he's super gnarly and he only wants to follow the rules the exact way they're supposed to be followed. So now the uncle's the king and he bosses everyone around. He says that only one of the dead brothers can be buried 'cause he was a good guy and the other dead brother guy can't be buried 'cause he was a traitor. So he says the traitor brother guy has to be left in the street to rot and stink up the place.

Well, the two dead brothers have a sister named Antigone, and she thinks the whole thing is *totally* messed up 'cause she wants *both* of her brothers to be buried. She doesn't care about any of the stupid rules that say traitors can't be buried and they have to be left out in the street to rot. After all, even if her brother was a traitor he's still her brother and who wants to see their dead brother lying on the side of the road all dead with flies landing on him and stuff? So she sneaks out at night and puts a little dust on her dead, unburied, traitor-guy brother. She, like, buries him halfway or something.

So the king's super mad 'cause she broke "the rule." So he says even though they're related and he's her uncle and everything, he's still the king and she *has* to play by the rules. He says she has to *die* if she doesn't keep her mouth shut and knock it off, but she doesn't, she sneaks out and buries him *again,* so the king . . . he sentences her to death.

At the end of the stupid story practically everyone's dead. I mean the king's nephews, his niece, his wife, his son *all croak.* The only one who makes it to the end is the king dude. He made sure that everyone followed the rules, but in the end he loses everything. It's a stupid story if you ask me.

Finally the bell rings and it's time for lunch. I walk out of class with Erin. I tell her I think the whole story is messed up and confusing and lame, but she tells me she likes it. She likes Antigone anyway 'cause she's kinda gnarly—she stands up for what she thinks is right and she doesn't care what anyone else thinks. She doesn't take people's crap. I see what she means, but I still think the stupid story is way too hard to understand.

Erin goes off with her group and I meet Brendon at our usual lunch spot. When he finally shows up we eat our lunch and talk about skating. He talks me into going to Old Oaks bowl with him after school for a session. I'd rather skate the half-pipe at the skate park, but whatever. I just want to skate, so I agree to give Old Oaks a try.

After school I wait a long time for stupid Brendon to show up so we can go skate. I almost bail, but then I see him dip around the corner. "Where were you, ya moron?" I ask.

He looks at me with narrow eyes and kicks an empty chocolate milk carton into the bushes. "Sitting in Buttcrack's office."

"Whaddya do?"

"Nothing."

"Come on. Whaddya do?"

"I didn't do anything," he says. "Buttcrack's hassling me about grades again, says he wants to talk to me and my mom and stuff . . . that I'll have to go to Sunrise High . . . Whatever, I'm over it . . . let's go skate."

He whips around and heads down the long, gum-stained concrete path toward the gates of our school. He's clutching his skateboard by the trucks; it dangles at his side and he's walking so fast toward the exit, he's practically running. I catch up and walk next to him. I don't say anything even though I want to. I wanna say quit being a jackass. I wanna say don't flunk out of high school 'cause you're really smart. I wanna say don't leave me here in this place alone 'cause you're my best friend and I don't wanna be here without you. I wanna say why can't things be like they were? But of course . . . I don't say anything . . . I'm stoic. We hop on our boards and skate off.

12

INITIATION

The setup at Old Oaks is sweet! There's a small, three-foot-high cement bowl shaped like an ashtray, with this buttery curved coping that runs along the top for tailslides and stuff. It has, like, three sets of stairs and a little mini ramp built into it too. It's in the corner of the park, and right next to it is the playground with swings and a grass field where kids and dogs can play and everything. There's a basketball court right next to the bowl, which is sweet 'cause it's really smooth, flat concrete. Sometimes skaters bring rails and boxes and stuff and set it up in the basketball court. I can't believe they built a place to skate that's free. I think they made it 'cause they thought that little kids would use it. I guess they had no idea that it would be mobbed by every skater in our town. Anyway, the worst thing about it is it gets really crowded, so the people who skate there all the time think they own it or something. But the afternoon Brendon and me skate, it isn't too bad.

Brendon totally has the place wired. He pulls this crazy trick. He does this nollie big spin over the three stair into the bowl and then does this sick backside tailslide along the coping. He knows a lot more guys at the bowl than me and they all give him high fives and stuff. I have a good time busting indys out of the bowl. I ollie over the stairs into the bowl and pull 50–50s along the coping a few times. The concrete feels so smooth, it doesn't make that clackity sound like at the skate park.

I want to go for one more run, but some big guy named Junior sits on the ledge with his legs dangling over, resting right in the sweetest part of the bowl. He has on sunglasses and his head is shaved. He starts smoking a cigarette and it doesn't look like he's planning on leaving anytime soon. I decide I'm done skating, so I tell Brendon let's head across the highway to the liquor store and get a cold drink. We sit on the curb outside the store. I put my cold bottle of root beer against my sweaty forehead. Brendon takes a chug of his drink and then starts playing with a hole in the toe of his shoe. He looks over at me.

"How come you don't try anything new?" he asks.

I shrug. "I don't know . . . I like root beer."

"No, that's not what I'm talking about. Like, when we skate . . . ollies, 50–50s—same tricks every time . . . Just seems like it would get moldy after a while."

"But I like those tricks," I say.

I gotta go home 'cause I have a ton of homework and I tell Brendon he might want to think about doing a little homework too. He laughs and says he's gonna go skate some more at the bowl. And he will. He'll skate till dark and then go home and sit around and watch reruns of *The Simpsons*. He's such a pile!

Finally Friday comes and I'm stoked. Brendon's gonna spend the whole weekend at my house. We decide to go for a gonzo skate session at night, so we hit the pavement just after dark. At this one spot behind the Thrifty Save shopping center, there's these sick concrete ledges and a killer gap—super sick for skating. We go there and it's quiet and the lights give it this kind of creepy, cool glow and there's nobody around. Perfect.

Brendon climbs up on the ledge and runs as fast as he can toward the gap. He drags his board by the nose, wheel-side down next to him, then he drops it and hops on. He's going super fast. He pops the tail, slides his feet forward, and pulls his knees to his chest. His arms are spread out like a giant bird and it's like he has magnets on his feet or something. He sails over the gap with his board glued to the bottom of his feet and you can see his flying shadow against the massive back wall of the Thrifty Save. He lands it and keeps rolling.

Brendon skies over the gap a bunch more times and in the meantime I pile up a bunch of these wood plank pallet things and make this cool mini launch ramp and I start skating too. After a while I get tired so I kick back on my board and watch Brendon and his shadow go for one more run. He skates over to where I'm sitting and sits on his board too. We both start chipping little pieces of wood from the pallets and try to make mini skateboards or stuff that'll fly.

"Hey, Brendon, you talked to Erin lately?" I ask.

"Yeah, every day. She doesn't know it yet, but she's gonna be my girl."

"She's super smart."

"You mean super hot . . . I swear . . . she could be in a magazine if she wanted."

"She's super cool too."

"For sure, she could be." Brendon tosses a mini wooden airplane thingy he made out of chipped wood into the air, but it doesn't fly. He stands up. "Hey, let's bail. Let's get outta here."

So we leave. I'm thinking we should head over to Federico's for some tasty grub, but we skate around this one corner and that's when we see it. It's one of those golf cart things that the security guards use to patrol the shopping center. There's nobody around and the keys are in it. Brendon looks at me and smiles. I stand there shaking my head. "No way, dude . . . we're gonna get in trouble . . . *you're* gonna get me in trouble. *Please* let's just go eat!" He throws his board in the back and hops into the driver's seat. "Quit being a grandma," he says. "Get in."

I know there is no way I'm gonna talk him out of this, so I hop in next to him. Brendon grabs the steering wheel and floors it.

We lurch forward like the Dukes of Hazzard or something, buzzing through the Thrifty Save shopping center all fast and furious. We careen around a corner and get the thing up on two wheels. We laugh and hoot and holler. We drive it back to where we were skating and try to launch off the mini ramp I built with those pallet things. Brendon floors it, we race toward the ramp, but as soon as our front wheels hit we hear the wood crack, pop, and splinter and pieces of wood explode out from underneath us, flying everywhere. "Holy crap!" I holler. We screech to a stop and I'm laughing so hard I feel like I'm gonna pee my pants. I look over and Brendon's laughing too, cracking up. His head is tilted back and he's slapping the steering wheel.

"It's our fat butts, dude, it's our big, fat butts!" he screams and laughs at the same time. Then we hear a loud voice echo against the back wall of the Thrifty Save.

"Stop right there!" We look over and see an old man security guard beaming his flashlight in our direction. He's got a ball cap sitting way up high on his head, a bushy gray mustache, and a belly that looks like he swallowed a giant watermelon or something. He starts walking over our way all bowlegged and stuff and he looks mad . . . super mad.

"Crap," Brendon blurts out. He puts the golf cart in reverse, but the stupid thing won't budge 'cause a piece of wood is lodged underneath the front axle. The guard starts running toward us and screaming into his walkie-talkie, "I got 'em, I got 'em . . . send backup *now!* " So we grab our boards, jump out of the golf cart, and start running and that old man security guard runs after us. He yells into his walkie-talkie and he's talking all that cop stuff that they use on TV, "I'm on foot, in pursuit, blah, blah, blah," and I'm practically crapping my pants 'cause he's a pretty fast runner for a grandpa and he's so close I can hear him breathing. I'm afraid he's gonna reach out his arm and grab me, but then the adrenaline kicks in and I really start to move.

"Josh . . . fence," Brendon screams. We scurry up this six-foot wall, hurl our boards over this super-high chain-link fence, and start climbing. We land on the other side of the fence and look back. The old man knows he's beat—he doesn't even try to chase us now—he just stands at the fence yelling into his walkie-talkie and then we hear police sirens. Brendon and me look at each other and bolt. We run to these apartment buildings that are behind the Thrifty Save and dive into some bushes underneath the stairs. We're lying on our stomachs with our heads down, breathing super hard, and my heart's beating so fast I can hear it booming in my head. Finally I catch my breath.

"Holy crap, dude . . . If we get caught I'm ruined," I whisper.

"We're not gonna get caught."

"My life's over."

"We're not gonna get caught, Josh, just relax, wouldya?"

"If I get caught my parents are gonna—"

"Shut up! Someone's coming."

"Crap," I whisper into my arm.

A bunch of footsteps clomp around on the concrete walkways and we both lie super still. Then a couple of guys come in our direction. I see the treads of their black boots as they pass by, the beams of their flashlights moving all around. All I can hear is my breathing and the way those guys squeak and rattle when they walk 'cause of all that cop stuff they're wearing on their belts. I tighten every muscle in my body and hold my breath. Finally I hear a deep voice say, "No one here," and the footsteps fade off into the distance. It's quiet. I exhale.

We stay there for like five minutes and then we hear their cars start up and pull away. We slowly climb out from the bushes, brush the fronts of our hoodies off, and grab our boards. Brendon has dried leaves in his hair and he's smiling.

"Dude, that was *so sick!*"

"Dude, that was *sketchy!*" I say.

"Did you see that security guard? He thought he had us. He was *so* pissed."

"That *was* pretty sick! I can't *believe* we didn't get caught."

"See, dude, you should try new things every once in a while . . . live a little."

"Whatever. Let's go home," I say.

"No way! Let's go skate," and he hops on his board and starts heading toward Old Oaks Park. "Crap," I whisper under my breath 'cause I know Brendon—I know that when he puts his mind to something, there's no stopping him, so I do the only thing I can do—I hop on my board and follow.

When we get to Old Oaks bowl no one's there. It's kinda cool 'cause it's all dark and glowy and the stars are out and stuff. It's empty except for me and Brendon. All I can hear is a car pass by every once in a while. It's kinda peaceful and I need to chill out so I lie down on the damp grass next to the bowl and check out the stars while Brendon does flip tricks off the stairs. I can hear my heart beating, and it's calmer now. I'm about to peel myself from the grass and start skating the bowl when we hear something—a whistle from the shadows. We look behind us and Lenny and Junior saunter over from the picnic tables. Junior's still wearing sunglasses even though it's night and Lenny has a bandanna wrapped around his head and an unlit cigarette lodged from where the bottom half of his front tooth used to be.

"Hey—what are you doing here at night? This is our park—we'll slit your throats if we don't like ya," Lenny says. He laughs and slaps Junior on the shoulder. Brendon skates right up to them, shakes their hands, and starts talking. I hear Lenny, trying to be all tough and cool and stuff. "Who's your little friend over there?" he says.

"Josh, come over here," Brendon shouts my way. I sigh and skate over.

"What's up?" I nod at Lenny and Junior and then look at the ground. Lenny takes a lighter out of his pocket, lights his cigarette, takes a drag. He's looking right at me. Brendon tells him about the whole golf cart thing—about how the security guard chased us and how we almost got rolled by the cops. Lenny turns his head and spits. "Sounds like you two boys are looking for some real action," he says, still staring right at me, "Hey, Lowman, you want to get initiated—you and Brendon here?" I have no idea what he's talking about.

"What?" I say.

"You and Brendon, you go over to the liquor store and get us some beer."

"But we're not old enough."

"No duh . . . you get us some beer, ya know . . . for free."

"You mean steal it?"

"You get us some beers and then you're initiated. You can skate the bowl whenever you want. If anyone ever hassles you . . . you got backup."

But it doesn't sound like such a great deal to me 'cause the only person I ever need backup *from* is Lenny and his pack of hyenas. Lenny pushes me in the arm and says, "Whaddya say, Lowman? You in? Junior's getting thirsty and so am I." I look over at Brendon. He's got his hands in his pockets and he's looking down at his skateboard. I'm tired and I've already been chased by the cops once tonight.

"Naw . . . I'm out. I'm going home," I say.

Lenny looks over at Brendon. "How 'bout you—you gonna man up or you gonna be a little wuss like this pile of crap here?"

Brendon looks up from his board and looks at me. *Don't do it, don't do it, Brendon,* I try to tell him with my eyes. He turns and looks at Lenny and I hear him mutter the words, "I'm in . . ." I can't believe it. I don't even hear what they say to him, but I see them give him high fives and slap him on the shoulder. I faintly hear the words, "Later, Josh," and then the three of them turn around and disappear into the shadows. I feel like I'm in some kind of a bad dream or something. I'm standing in the middle of Old Oaks Park. I'm alone and cold and hungry and tired. I see Brendon and Lenny and Junior's dark shadows slink across the highway and slip behind the liquor store. I just want to go to bed. I hop on my board and skate home underneath the streetlights. All I can hear is the sound of my wheels hitting the cracks in the sidewalk. It echoes through the neighborhood and disappears into the night.

13

SOLO

Brendon never showed up all weekend. On Monday I swing by our meeting spot at lunch, but I don't see him and I don't wait around. I head over to the lunch tables and sit with Cody and Niko, these freshman guys I know from the skate park. I see Erin and a couple of her friends sitting at a table with Danny Ramsey and a bunch of other jocks. She looks over at me and waves. I sit there and eat my lunch and Cody and Niko and me talk about skating. Cody and Niko have never dropped in from the top of the vert ramp; they're just like me—they have to start at the bottom and work their way up the sides. They're gonna skate after school and we decide to meet at the vert ramp to work on our skills. I wish I was skating right now. I wish I didn't have to go to *three more stupid classes* before I'm free.

When I get to the skate park, Cody and Niko are already there. I see them standing at the top of the vert ramp. I slap on my helmet, grab my board, and book up the stairs. When I get to the top we all stand at the edge and stare down into the belly of the beast.

"You gonna drop in?" I ask.

Cody says, "Not today."

Niko keeps looking down the vert ramp, studying the drop. He shakes his head.

"Nope," he says.

"Me neither," I say, and we head down the stairs and go over to mini land.

We skate for a long time. Drop in on the ramps and practice tricks and stuff. After a while we head back over to the vert ramp. We take turns starting from the bottom and pumping up the walls to see who can get the highest. I go first.

I start off slow. I go up about four feet on one side, kickflip around, pump my board through the bottom of the ramp, and inch up the other side. I'm gaining speed and with each pump I get a little bit higher up the sides. I can hear Cody and Niko hooting and egging me on and stuff. Pretty soon I'm like two feet from the very top and I don't bail or anything. I totally handle it, I'm in total control.

Pretty soon my legs get tired. I bail onto my knees and slide down to the bottom. When I finally stop sliding, I lie down at the bottom of the vert ramp spread-eagle. I look up into the sky and smile. Cody and Niko run over and help me up. They slap me on the shoulder. "Dude that was sick!" they both scream. They each take their turns and they get super high up the walls of the vert ramp too. We decide it's a three-way tie and I'm stoked 'cause it's the highest I've ever gotten on the beast.

I have to leave an hour before the skate park closes 'cause I have to go to stupid tutoring. My mom drives me and we go by Old Oaks Park. I don't even bother to look over and see the skaters. Instead, I review the chapter in my math book that I have a test on tomorrow. When I get to the tutoring place Zander's waiting for me in the math lab. Before we go over all of this lame math stuff, I tell him about the vert ramp. I tell him how I was almost to the

top, that I could practically reach out my hand and touch the coping. I tell him I wish math was cool and fun, like skating. And you
know what he says? He says skaters are naturals at math 'cause
they're used to looking at things in different ways. Then he points
out the window to the entrance of the building. "What do you
see?" he asks.

"I don't know—stairs and stuff. Totally sick for skating."

"Why?"

"'Cause you could jump 'em. Jump the stairs or skate the
handrails down to the bottom. That'd be sick!"

He points. "And what about those cement planter box things
over there?"

"Sweet ledges. You could totally tailslide and grind those . . . you
could do a bunch of different flip tricks on those," I say. "Too bad
we're in here and not out there skating."

Zander smiles. "I know, but that's not the point."

"Well, then what is, besides math sucking."

"The point is, what does your mom see when she looks out this
window? Or your dad? What do people who don't skate see when
they look out these windows?"

I think about it for a second. "I guess they see stairs and
handrails and planter boxes."

"Exactly! You're a skater. You see things in a different way. That's
math."

I don't always understand everything that Zander says, especially
when he starts talking like Yoda and stuff, but I like him . . . he's
cool. So I sit there and listen to him talk some more. He says that
there's all kinds of math in skating—180s, 360s—that ramps are
like triangles lying down on their side and half-pipes are cylinders

cut in half and stuff like that . . . and I start thinking, Zander knows a lot about math, but he knows a lot about skateboarding too.

"Come on Zander, tell me the truth. Do you skate?" I ask.

He smiles and nods. "Skated vert today, before I got here . . . Mountain View Skate Park . . . it's close to my college."

I can't believe it! Zander's the first really smart skater I ever met. I mean, I thought only jocks and nerds and my sister went to college and here's Zander airing out of vert ramps and probably studying some kind of super-hard rocket science or something. He laughs when I tell him I didn't think skaters were the college type and all. He says that skaters get a bum rap sometimes 'cause a lot of people think we're hoodlums, but we're not . . . that there's all kinds of skaters, good guys and hoodlums too, just like there's all kinds of jocks. And then he tells me that some of his skater friends are dudes he goes to college with, that they're super-sick skaters and really smart, some of the most creative, talented people he knows.

"You're lucky," I say, "'cause most of the skaters I know, the super-sick, really good skaters that hang out around here—most of them are dirtbags."

He nods. "Yep, there *are* dirtbags, but there are a lot of smart people too." Then he stops talking about skating and makes me focus on algebra. By the time we're finished, I feel ready to take that stupid algebra test in Mr. Snoggins's class. I'm ready for battle! I'm ready to slay the beast!

14

GRACE IS SICK

At school today I walk by me and Brendon's meeting spot and he's sitting there waiting for me. He doesn't say anything about what happened on Friday night after he bailed on me and I don't ask, but I can tell he feels kinda bad or something 'cause he asks me if I wanna skate the skate park later on this afternoon. So we go to the skate park. Brendon spends all his time on the street course. I hang out and skate with him for a while, but then I get bored so I head over to the half-pipe. After we're done skating he invites himself over to my house for dinner, which is fine with me 'cause my mom likes to feed him . . . she says the only proper nutrition Brendon gets is when he eats at our house.

After dinner we go outside. We're skating down my driveway when we hear the neighbor's dog barking really loud. Brendon looks at me. "Dude, I saw this thing on TV last night. Did you know a dog can smell fear . . . it can like sense that you're afraid of it and stuff, and if it senses that you're afraid, or it feels threatened . . . that's when it bites."

"But what if you are afraid?" I ask.

"I don't know. You just have to pretend that you're not afraid and then you won't get bit."

We skate in the street in front of my house until it's almost dark.

Before he leaves, Brendon says he's gonna skate Old Oaks tomorrow after school and asks me if I want to come along. I tell him maybe and then my mom hollers at me from the house that it's time to come in and start my homework. I tell Brendon later and turn around and walk up the driveway.

"Hey, Josh," he says. I turn around and he looks at me for a second. "Nevermind." He hops on his board and skates away under the buzzing, flickering streetlights.

The next day I see Brendon at school. He asks me if I wanna skate the bowl with him later on and you know what? . . . I don't feel like skating over there today, I'd rather skate with Niko and Cody over at the skate park, so I tell Brendon some other time. Then I tell him about Zander. I tell him that Zander's this really smart, math guy skater dude and that sometimes he thinks he's Yoda. I tell him about that time he made me take a skateboard apart to teach me the order of operations. Brendon laughs and says he sounds really weird. We start talking about the golf cart and the security guard and the cops and hiding in the bushes and for a second it's like we're back in seventh grade again. Then the stupid bell rings. I walk in the direction of my next class and when I turn around to tell Brendon something, he's heading toward the gate.

The next day in English class, Erin asks me where Brendon's been 'cause she's talked to him on the phone a bunch but she hasn't seen him around school very much. I tell her I think he's lost and she laughs. "I'm meeting him at Old Oaks Park tomorrow. You gonna be there?" she asks. But we have to be quiet 'cause Ms. Moreland starts talking about all this stupid English stuff she tells us is important.

I see Brendon at lunch the next day and he asks me if I wanna skate with him after school again. I think maybe he's starting to miss me. I tell him I'll go as long as I don't get in the way of his hot hookup with Erin. "Whatever," he says and smiles. When we first get to Old Oaks, only a few guys are skating. It's a perfect afternoon. I take a few turns dropping in on the bowl and 50–50 grind along the coping. When I look over, Erin's cruising down the sidewalk. She cuts across the grass and goes and sits under a tree. Brendon's busy on the flat, smooth concrete of the basketball court, working on a flip trick he saw on a skate video. He nods and smiles at her. She doesn't see me.

I pop my board up into my hand and walk across the grass. When I get to where she's sitting, she's reading a book. She doesn't look up or anything—it's like she's in her own little world. She kinda chews on her bottom lip and runs her fingers along her forehead, sweeping some hair behind her ear. She doesn't even know I'm there, so I just stand there for a second all quiet and then I knock on my skateboard. "Hello, anybody home?" She looks up. The grass makes her green eyes even greener, and in the sunlight they look all sparkly and stuff. She smiles at me.

"Hey Josh," she says. I say hi and sit down next to her.

"Whaddya reading?" I ask.

"Some book I found in the library . . . mythology."

I nod. "Mythology . . . those are those crazy stories about guys who fought monsters with octopus arms and lion's tails and stuff, right?"

"Yeah, and all the gods cheat on each other and gossip and fall in love with mortals and stuff." She reaches across her book and picks a piece of grass.

"That would totally suck to have to battle some crazy monster with three heads and a giant eye and a bunch of arms and stuff," I say.

"Yeah, guess you're right." She flicks a piece of grass into the air and watches it flutter to the ground. "This book says they made up all those stories . . . like how the world started, and things about the gods and stuff 'cause they were looking for answers," she says.

"Answers?"

"Yeah, answers . . . I mean, it's not like they could open a book and figure out why it rains or why there's lightning. They made up stories 'cause they wanted things to make sense."

I look at her sideways.

"You know . . . the gods are sad, they cry, so it rains—they're mad so they throw lightning from the sky. They were just trying to understand things . . . And I kinda get that . . . I mean . . . don't you wish that things just made more sense sometimes?"

"Totally, I totally wish things made more sense," I say.

Erin sits up. She puts her book in her bag and lies on her side. Her head rests in her hand. "What about you? What do you like to read?"

"Me? Nothing!"

"Come on. Books are cool. There has to be something."

"*Books? Cool?* Are you feeling all right?"

"No, come on there has to be one book," she says.

"Do comics and skate mags count?"

"No . . . I'm talking about books, no pictures. What's your favorite book that you've ever read in your whole life?"

I sit there and think about it. I put a blade of grass between my teeth, chew the end into tiny pieces, and spit it out. "Do you promise you won't laugh?" I say.

"Of course I won't. What's your favorite book?"

"Well . . . when I was in seventh grade . . . we had to pick a book we wanted to read and do this stupid report thing on it, and I picked *Where the Red Fern Grows*. I was really mad at first that I had to do the stupid project, but I wound up really liking that book."

"I never read it."

"You should. It's about this kid and his two dogs and they go out hunting every night and stuff. And the boy and his dogs, they're like best friends, best friends in the whole world—his dogs, they'll do anything for him . . . they even die for him."

"Wow, sounds like a good book."

"It is. You should read it sometime . . . You'd like it."

We sit there for a few minutes, picking the grass and playing with it, twirling it in our fingers, throwing it into the breeze, watching it float and twirl until it lands on the ground and stuff. Then we notice Brendon skating. His arms are stretched out like wings. He flies through the air, his board right underneath him. He lands on the metal rail, floats across it, lands on the pavement, and keeps rolling. Erin says, "Do you promise you won't laugh?"

"Yeah, I promise," I say.

"He's beautiful when he skates, isn't he?"

"Who?"

"Brendon."

"You think Brendon's beautiful?'

"Well . . . yeah . . . kinda . . . when he's skating."

I shake my head. "No, you mean he's sick, he's a sick skater. That's what you're trying to say."

"No, that's not what I mean . . . that's not what I mean at all. I mean, he's beautiful when he skates. He's so graceful and he's in total control. He makes it look . . . pretty, like he's a bird or something. He's just really graceful, that's what I'm saying."

"Hmm . . . graceful . . ." I rest my chin in my hand. "It just sounds funny, I mean maybe a little girlie, don't ya think? I mean, what guy wants to be called graceful?"

Erin looks at me with her sparkly green eyes. "But graceful's good, Josh. Grace is a good thing, especially when you're moving. Wouldn't you rather be called graceful instead of clumsy or spastic or something?"

"I guess so . . . I guess you're right . . . grace is good. Grace is sick!" I say and we both laugh.

Brendon comes over to where we're sitting. His shirt's hanging out of his back pocket and his hair is all sweaty and stuff. He flops down next to Erin. The three of us sit there laughing and joking around. I get up and skate the bowl.

When I look over Brendon has his hand on Erin's hip. She takes his hand and puts it on the grass and he puts his hand back on her hip and they start laughing. I drop into the bowl a few more times before I head over to where Erin and Brendon are sitting. I tell them I have to bail and Erin says she's gotta go too. She stands up, brushes the grass off her butt, grabs her stuff, and waves goodbye. I grab my skateboard and head home. When I turn around and look back, I see Brendon flying over a rail, arms stretched out like a gliding bird . . . graceful.

15

OBSCURE

We have a new word of the day in English class. Ms. M. writes the word OBSCURE in big black letters on the whiteboard and then she writes the definition next to it, but before anyone can see it, she tapes a piece of paper over half of the word she wrote. Then she turns around and asks us why the definition is hidden. I say, "'Cause you're crazy," and the whole class laughs, even Ms. Moreland. She says I'm right, that she *is* crazy, but that's not why she covered up some of the definition. She asks if there's anyone else who wants to guess, but no one raises their hand. She walks up to the whiteboard and takes the piece of paper down. It turns out *obscure* means partially hidden, which I don't totally get, so I'm glad that she explains it a little more. She says that something is obscure when things are kind of unclear and so you don't really understand what they mean.

Finally, Ms. M. stops talking about vocabulary and we start reading that stupid play *Antigone* from where we left off at the last class. She picks me to read the part of the uptight uncle, so whenever my part comes along, I read it in this really deep serious voice. The whole class kinda laughs, even Ms. M., she starts laughing too, 'cause you know . . . it's funny. She doesn't get mad, or freak out or have a spaz attack or anything, she just says that I'm reading it "in character" and even though it sounds funny, it's probably the way my character would talk. At least Ms. M. doesn't try and get you in trouble when you're just trying to have a little fun. So we keep reading the play and finally the bell rings.

I meet Brendon at our lunch spot. He's sitting there eating a nasty burrito that he bought from the school cafeteria. I take out some logos I've been working on for our skate company and we check 'em out. We both agree that the one of the skating burrito is the sickest. So we sit there, eating our lunch, hanging out, not bothering a fly, when Vice Principal Bedcraft has to walk over and ruin everything. "Mr. Johnson," he says. He calls Brendon "Mr. Johnson." What a dork! "Mr. Johnson," he says, "I'm happy to see you here at school. Have you been going to all of your classes lately?" So of course Brendon says, "Yeah, I've been going." And then Buttcrack walks away and leaves us alone.

We sit there and it's quiet. Brendon tears off pieces of the gold paper his burrito was wrapped in, rolls them into tiny little balls, and flicks them into the air. I watch them arc through the sky, hit the gum-speckled concrete, and roll into the bushes. "Buttcrack's a jerk," I say.

Brendon nods in agreement. He stands up, crunches the rest of the wrapper into a ball, and tosses it on the ground.

"I'm not going here anymore," he says, "I'm over it." And then all cool and calm and collected, he tells me he's gonna quit going to our school at the end of the semester—that him and his mom talked about it and he's already made his decision. He says he wants to go to a school where there's more "freedom" and where people like Buttcrack aren't totally on your case all the time. I can't believe it. I sit there thinking, *What about our company? What about*

Maximum Brotherhood? But before the words even come out he says it'll be easier to start a company if one of us has sponsors. Then he turns and looks at me.

"You know, Sunrise isn't only for losers. You can go there and graduate too and everything," he says. And I look at him, but I don't say anything. He asks me if I want to skate Old Oaks after school, and I mumble something like "too much homework," 'cause my stomach feels weird and for some reason, I'm not in the mood to skate.

When I get home I go straight to my bedroom. I lie on my bed staring at the poster of Danny Way airing over the wall of China that hangs on my wall, when I hear a knock on my door. It's my mom. She comes in and sits on the edge of my bed. She asks me what's wrong and I tell her I don't feel so hot. She puts her hand on my forehead and says she thinks I might have a low fever, nothing too serious, but she's worried just the same. And I can't really explain it exactly. I'm not sure if it's my head, or my stomach, or both. I just feel funny and that's what I tell my mom. She takes a good look at me and tells me to get some rest.

She leaves my room, comes back in and puts a cool, wet washcloth on my forehead, then goes downstairs. I hear her rustling around and when my dad gets home from work I hear 'em talking. She tells him I'm not feeling well, probably the flu or something, that I'll probably stay home from school tomorrow. Fine with me. I lie there, not really sure what's going on. My head feels super heavy, my stomach feels all weird and tingly and stuff, and I can hear my heart thumping in my head. I feel all drowsy. I lie there and eventually I drift off to sleep.

I stay home the next day and I'm happy to not have to sit

through six hours of torture at school. The only problem is I know I'm gonna have a ton of makeup work when I get back. Those teachers, they don't give you a break. You could be in the hospital with pneumonia or something, gasping for your last breath of air, and they'd still find a way to get work out of you. I swear, they're like bloodsuckers or something. So anyway, in the afternoon after school is out, I call Cody to find out what I missed in math. I don't ask him to, but Cody comes over to my house and gives me the notes he took, which is totally cool.

We sit down at our big table in the kitchen and spread all our stuff out. I copy the half page of notes that Mr. Snoggins gave in class today and then Cody starts to explain what they mean, and guess what? Cody's a really good explainer. We sit there, finishing our math homework together. I get a couple wrong answers, but Cody, he gets them all right.

I tell Cody how much I hate math, how it's such a waste of time and how we're never gonna use it in our whole lives, so why do we have to waste our time learning the stupid stuff. And I think he's gonna feel the exact same way, that we're gonna open a Math Haters Club at Valley View High and it's gonna be the most popular club at school. But guess what he says? He says he thinks math is kinda *cool*. Can you believe it? He thinks math is cool 'cause it's *clear* once you understand it . . . it's *clear,* and there's a *right answer.* You're either right or not—there's nothing in between 'cause with math, you kinda know where you stand. I can't believe it. I thought everyone hated math, except Zander.

"Besides, I'm gonna need math when I'm older 'cause I'm gonna build skateparks," he says.

"Skate parks?" I tilt my head.

"Think about it . . . Somebody's gotta build 'em. That's what I'm gonna do. I'm gonna go to college and study architecture or engineering or something, and I'm gonna build super-sick skate parks all over the world."

And I can totally see it. I mean, I can picture Cody when he's older and all. He's with a crew of burly construction workers leaning over a big set of building plans and he has a pencil behind his ear. He wears one of those big yellow hard hats that has a sick logo of a burrito with wings on a skateboard, and he points to the blueprints, explaining to the workers how they're gonna build his ramps and stuff. Totally sick!

"I could be your tester or something," I say.

He looks at me like I'm crazy. "Tester?" he asks.

"Yeah, your tester, 'cause before you could let anyone skate on the stuff you build, you would need to know if it works, right? I could be the guy who comes in and skates your ramps, tests them out in case you need to make some adjustments or something. That's gonna be my company. That's what I'm gonna do. I'm gonna be a ramp specialist tester dude."

We laugh. Then we clear our stuff from the table and Cody splits. When we eat dinner my mom asks me about Cody, who he is and stuff. "He's my friend." I tell her. I eat my soup and I'm happy 'cause my stomach isn't all tingly and my head doesn't feel funny anymore.

The next day I see Erin in English class. We have to do these super-lame presentations where we have to get up in front of the whole class and act out a scene from *Antigone*. We even have to wear these toga things 'cause that's what those ancient old guys wore back in the old days. And to make it even worse we have to rewrite our scene in our own words so that it's not so hard to understand. So Erin and I are doing the part where the uncle gets really mad at Antigone for breaking the rules and he tells her to knock it off, and it's written so long ago, and the words are so jumbly and weird, that I don't even see why we have to read the stupid thing.

"What's the point of this story anyway?" I say.

And Erin looks up from her paper and looks at me for a second, and I think she's gonna say something like *Yeah, I know, it's so lame.* But instead she says, "I'm not totally sure, but I think it's about winning and losing."

I look at her with a totally blank stare.

"Well, Antigone stands up for what she believes in, you know, she does what she thinks is right, so even though she dies, she still wins."

I shake my head. "That's a bunch of crap, she doesn't win . . . she croaks," I say.

"But she still wins."

"No way. She's dead. She loses. Nobody wins. I mean, what about the uncle? He gets *totally* burned. He follows all the rules and at the end of the story, he loses everything. He does what he thinks is right but he loses! See, I hate this play. It's so stupid. You break the rules, you die. You follow the rules you lose. Everybody loses. It's a *stupid* play!"

It's quiet for a second. Erin stares at the piece of paper lying in front of her, and then she looks at me. "Maybe that's the whole point . . . maybe sometimes you have to make up your own rules, do what you think is right, then no matter what, you win, no matter what other people say."

"Whatever." I tear off the corner of my paper and wad it up into a tiny ball. "It's a stupid play . . . impossible to understand . . . I hate it."

Just then Ms. Moreland walks over to where we're sitting so we both shut up and start working on our scripts. Finally she walks away.

"Hey, Erin," I say, "do you think you can be really graceful at some things but really lame at other stuff?"

"I'm not sure I know what you mean . . ."

"Brendon's dropping out. Says he's transferring to Sunrise High next semester."

She doesn't say a word. She just looks at me then down at her paper.

"Hey," she says, "we're not gonna finish our scene in time. Can you meet me at Old Oaks Park this afternoon? You can skate if you want, then we can work on our scripts for a little bit." At first I say no, but she talks me into it. So we agree to meet at the park after school.

16

STUPID SHOES

When I get to Old Oaks I throw my backpack under a tree and walk across the grass toward the bowl. I see Brendon. He's skating a rail that somebody set up on the flat pavement of the basketball court. He looks up, nods at me, and skates over. We take turns skating the bowl together—first Brendon, then me—we don't talk much, just skate, which is the way we both like it. Then we see Erin walk over to my backpack. She sits under the tree and waves. We both skate to the edge of the grass, kick our boards up into our hands, and cruise over to where she's sitting. We plop down on the ground next to her. The first thing she says is "Hey, Brendon, I hear you're dropping out of school." He shoots me a death stare, then picks a piece of grass and starts tearing it apart into little pieces.

"Yeah, I'm kinda over Valley View . . . the place is a hellhole . . . it's like a prison or something and they treat you like a baby." Erin just sits there all quiet. I can't take it anymore.

"But why . . . what're ya gonna do?" I ask.

"I'm gonna go to Sunrise Continuation, that's what I'm gonna do . . . I talked to a bunch of people over there and they say it's cool . . . way cool. All you have to do is show up and do the work and nobody hassles you."

I sit there and shake my head. "But that's the thing . . . you don't have to show up," I say. "That's the problem, it's like there's *too* much freedom and nobody cares if you don't show up."

My face gets kinda warmish and my heart starts to race. I'm waiting for Erin to help me out and say something super smart like she always does. I'm waiting for her to tell him that there's *too* much freedom . . . that it's *too* easy to get lost over there and people get stuck. They *say* they're gonna graduate and stuff but they don't. There's too much freedom and people get lost and then they're stuck forever. But she doesn't say a word. She sits on the green grass Indian-style, twirling the ends of her long brown hair around her fingers, studying Brendon and me like we're some kind of interesting book or something.

"You know, everyone thinks Sunrise's full of losers . . . that's what *everyone* thinks . . . I'm just tired of everyone telling me what to do, that's all. Buttcrack . . . his stupid rules. I'm over it. And besides, what's the big deal? It's not like a stupid high school diploma means anything anyway."

"I just don't understand why you're doing this," I say.

It's quiet. Brendon stares at the ground right in front of him, picking at the grass. I reach over, pick up a piece of grass, and start playing with it too. Erin looks at me, then at Brendon, then she finally says something. "You guys want to go to a party this weekend?" Both Brendon and me look at her. "Danny Ramsey's parents are out of town and he's having a party. He invited me and told me I could bring whoever I want," she says.

Brendon smiles. I stare at the foothills on the horizon and don't say a word. "For sure, me and Josh are there. It'll be my going-away party," he says and slaps me on the shoulder.

We stand up getting ready to leave when a car door slams. Someone whistles and calls Brendon's name. I look over and see my two favorite people in the whole world, Lenny and Junior. They saunter over to where we're standing and give Brendon a high five. Junior has a bandanna wrapped around his head sitting super low so you can barely see his eyes and Lenny has the stub of an unlit cigarette dangling from the space where his front tooth used to be. He doesn't say anything to me but he looks Erin up and down for a long time with a dumb grin on his ugly face.

"Who's your friend?" he asks.

"This is Erin," Brendon mutters.

Lenny flicks his cigarette on the ground. "Hel-lo Erin," he says. He looks at Junior and moves his eyebrows up and down on his stupid forehead a couple times. He reaches over, grabs Erin around the waist, and grinds his hips into hers, laughing.

I'm not sure what to do. I look at Brendon. He's just standing there so I just stand there too like an idiot. Erin pushes Lenny. "Stop." But he just pulls her closer. She knees him in the crotch but he jumps back before she makes contact.

"Whoa, settle down, now. Just having a little fun." Lenny smiles at Brendon and punches Junior in the arm.

"Let's get outta here, Erin," I say. I help her gather up her books, grab my skateboard, and we turn to leave.

"That's right, Lowlife, you two little princesses run along now," Lenny snarls, and he shoves me onto the sidewalk.

As we walk away I hear them laughing. I turn around to see what Brendon's doing. He doesn't say anything, not one word, he just stands there and looks down at his stupid shoes.

17

LITTLE TREMORS

Me and Erin meet in the library after school. Our stupid *Antigone* scene is due in English class in a few days and we haven't even written the script. We sit at a table and spread our things out. The library lady sits at her desk and reads the newspaper, and all the other kids sit around and talk and do homework. I'm playing the uncle in our scene so I have to make up what he says. "How about this," I tell Erin, and I speak in this really low voice. "Antigone, quit throwing dirt on your dead brother. I won't allow it, it's making me very angry!"

We both crack up and the library lady looks up from her newspaper and gives us a dirty look, which makes us crack up even more. And just then we hear this kind of quiet rumbling sound, real low like out of nowhere, and the books on our desk start to move around a little bit like they're dancing or something and the lights that are hanging from the ceiling start to squeak and swing back and forth real slow. We can feel our chairs kind of move around underneath us a little bit. I look at Erin and she looks at me. "What's that," I say.

"Earthquake," she says.

We look over at the lady, but she's disappeared under her desk and before we know it, it's over. Everyone sits there kind of quiet for a second and then the talking and laughing and homework start up again. The library lady gets back in her chair and tells us all to be quiet, that even though we just had a little tremor this is still a library and we have to use our library voices. Erin and I sit there for like an hour and we finally finish our scene. And I know Ms. Moreland and the whole class are going to like it because it's kind of funny, even though the play *Antigone* is supposed to be all heavy and dramatic and all, our scene is funny and I like it.

I'm upstairs in my room finishing my math homework when I hear my mom call me down. Brendon's at the door and he wants to know if I want to skate out front in the street before it gets dark. I'm almost done with all of my homework so my mom says it's okay. We're walking down my driveway when Brendon says real casual, like we're talking about the weather or something, he says, "My last day of school is this Friday—my mom signed the papers today. I start school at Sunrise Continuation on Monday." Just like that. I don't say anything, not one word. We're almost to the bottom of the driveway. "I was thinking we could go to that party Erin told us about. It'll be fun," he says. We stand at the bottom of the driveway for a second and look at the sky.

"Why do you hang out with them . . . Lenny . . . those guys . . . you're better than that," I say, and Brendon just stands there and looks at the ground.

He spins a wheel on his skateboard and we both stand there and watch it go around and around for a while. "Let's skate . . . let's just skate, okay?" he says, and he drops his board on the ground, puts a foot on it, and rolls it back and forth a few times. He looks down the street then up at the melting sun, hops on his board, and starts skating.

I stand there and watch him for a second, watch him bust an ollie. His board never leaves his feet; even when he's four feet up in the air his board is right underneath him. And that's the thing about Brendon—when he skates, he's fluid and free and natural, like he belongs flying through the air over a five-foot concrete gap, his board spinning underneath him, and everything is exactly the way it's supposed to be—perfectly natural. I stand there thinking, *How can a guy be so good at one thing, but totally suck at everything else? I mean, how can a guy be so in control of one part of his world while everything else spins out of control?* And I wish I had a bigger brain 'cause none of it makes any sense to me at all. So I get on my board and skate, me and Brendon, in the street, skating until the sun sets and the streetlights flicker on.

18

THE BIG ONE HITS

Brendon and I agree to meet at the party at around 8:30 PM. I want to go there with him, but for some reason he tells me we can't, so we decide to meet out front. I tell my mom I'm going to go skate for a while behind the Thrifty Save. I hop on my board and head over to Danny Ramsey's house and when I get there Erin's standing in the driveway. She comes out of the party to wait for me and Brendon so we stand there underneath the garage lights in Danny Ramsey's driveway waiting for Brendon to show up. I'm a little sweaty and the cool air feels good against my skin. I can hear the party going on in the background. Shouts and music and kids screaming and laughing float through the air. Erin and I lean up against the garage door and stand there for a while.

"Hey, remember the other day at the park?" I say. She doesn't look at me—she looks up from the ground, past the sidewalk, street, and houses, and stares out into the dark night sky. I don't know if she's listening or not, but I keep on talking. "I want you to know . . . I'm really sorry I just stood there. I mean Lenny's a jerk . . . a total jerk. You shouldn't have to listen to him or put up with any of his crap ever. I'm . . . I'm sorry I didn't do anything . . . I just . . . I didn't know what to do."

She looks at me for a second, she looks at me right in the eyes, and I guess she was listening 'cause real slowly she brings her hand up and puts it on my shoulder. "I'm glad you're my friend, Josh," she says, "you're a really good friend," and she leans in real close and kisses me on the cheek. Her lips feel smooth and soft and she smells good, like flowers. I look down at my shoes because I'm kind of embarrassed and I'm not really sure what to say, so I just tell her that I'm glad she's my friend too, and I totally mean it. I *am* glad she's my friend. She starts to walk away. She turns and tells me that when Brendon shows up to come and find her inside, that she needs to talk to him. She walks out from under the lights of the garage, turns the corner, and disappears through a side gate into the party.

And then I hear a voice—his voice. My heart drops and the hairs on the back of my neck stand up. It's Lenny. He slinks out from a bush into the garage light followed by Junior and Brendon. "Hey, Lowlife, what were you doing making out with Brendon's girlfriend?" he says. "We saw you—that's Brendon's girl, you little punk." I look at the ground. "Answer me, Lowlife, what were you doing with his chick? . . . What? . . . You too cool to talk to us? You think you're better than us? Go on . . . say something, pukeface."

I look up. "I wasn't *making out* with her. She's my *friend*."

"Don't get smart with me, you little lowlife punk," he says.

And before I can say something or do anything, Junior comes up behind me and locks my arms behind my back so I can't move. I'm standing there, wiggling and squirming, doing whatever I can to break free, and Lenny comes up to me and puts his face right in mine. His eyes are all red and glassy and he smells like beer and cigarettes. He stares at me for a long time. Then he growls, "You're nothing but a lowlife little punk." Spit flies into the air when he talks, like he's foaming at the mouth or something. I turn my face to the side. I can't stand the smell. I can't stand looking into his beady, bloodshot eyes. He punches me in the stomach a couple times and I feel like I'm going to puke. I yell at Brendon to help me, to make them stop, to do something, but he just stands there in a haze, his eyes all red and glazed over too.

And then . . . it's like everything moves in slow motion—Junior letting go of my arms . . . Lenny shoving me into the garage door . . . me, doubling over, holding my stomach, trying not to fall . . . Lenny picking up a skateboard, raising it over his head, swinging it around in the air with both hands, swinging it down with all his force like it's a sledgehammer. And there I am looking up just in time to see shiny metal trucks coming at me . . . hard metal on skull bone . . . a loud cracking thump ringing in my ears and then . . . nothing . . . lights out—everything goes black.

19

ICE CHIPS

I want to open my eyes, but I can't—they're just too heavy. I hear beeping and swishing and people's voices. I hear my mom and dad calling my name, feel them squeezing my hands. I want to open my eyes, but I can't, so I lie there a little bit longer. I slowly open my eyes, but I can't really focus on one thing. Everything's blurry. My eyelids float around on my eyeballs for a bit and I feel my mother's breath on my cheek. I see my father leaning over my bed, but it looks like he's under water. I hear my mom's voice. "Josh," she says, "Josh, sweetie, it's me, Mom, can you hear me." I try to nod my head but it feels like I have a bowling ball attached to my neck or something. I want to open my eyes, but I can't— they're just too heavy, so I don't. I close my eyes and go to sleep.

When my eyes finally flutter open I see my mom and dad sitting in the corner of the room. They hear me rustle around. They both pop out of their seats and come over to me. They grab my hand. "Are you all right?" "Thank God." They're crying, both of them crying and squeezing my hand. They look tired. I give them a weary smile. My eyes flutter open and close slowly. It's hard to talk. It feels like a semi truck drove down my windpipe. My mom takes a plastic spoon from a white Styrofoam cup and lifts it to my mouth. "Here, have some of these," she says, "it'll make your throat feel better." She slides something cold into my hot, dry mouth and I think *I just might be in heaven*. I don't know if I've ever had anything so good in my whole life . . . ice chips.

20

PASSING GAS

Do you know what's a funny thing about being in the hospital, like when you have an operation or something? The doctors and nurses and everyone don't think you're getting better until you fart. When I first wake up it seems like that's all anyone talks about. "How's your head? Did you get any sleep last night? Did you pass any gas?" And that's how they say it too—"passing gas." They want to let me try to stand up and walk around a little bit, since I haven't been out of bed in like six days or something, but first I have to fart. Whoopee! My mom and dad are in here all the time, every day, all day until they kick them out at 10 PM. My parents would even spend the night here if they could, but the nurses and doctors won't let them sleep over in the intensive care unit and that's where I am, the intensive care unit in the hospital, because this whole thing is intense . . . super intense . . . I think they should rename this part of the hospital the super-intense intensive care unit.

My mom and dad tell me I got conked on the head super hard and I got brought here in an ambulance and the doctors gave me a bunch of medicine and everything and I stayed asleep for like five days. I don't remember any of it, I mean, how I got to the hospital or anything, I just know that I have all these big white bandages wrapped around my head so that I look like some sort of a mummy or something. They have all these machines attached to me, and these nurses come in like every ten minutes to watch me breathe and to listen to my heart and everyone around here likes to talk about whether I've ripped a fart yet or not.

The best thing is, they let Erin in to see me, which is kind of cool 'cause they're super uptight around here about visitors and stuff. She brings me a couple of finger skateboards and a big card that says "Get well soon!" She sits next to my bed and we talk for a while. She tells me everyone in English class misses me and hopes I come back to school soon and that makes me feel kinda good and stuff.

Then she starts talking about the night of Danny Ramsey's party. She tells me how scared she was, how she was standing in Danny's backyard when some kid ran in and said that someone was passed out in front of the garage. Everyone came out to look and that's when Erin found me, lying there unconscious, in a pool of blood. She told Danny they needed to call an ambulance, call the police or something, but nobody wanted to. They wanted to just leave me lying there in the driveway I guess 'cause they were afraid the cops would come and bust up the party and Danny was afraid he would get in trouble. Erin yelled and screamed at everyone, but no one wanted to make the call, so she ran inside, grabbed a phone, and called 911 anyway. It's a good thing she did too 'cause I guess I was pretty messed up. I got hit on the head *so* hard that my brain got swollen. I didn't know your brain really could get bigger—get swollen and stuff—but it can and mine did, and they had to drill some holes in my head to let some of the air and pressure out and everything.

"Wow," I say to Erin. "Do you know who you were at that

party?" She looks at me with a weird expression on her face, shaking her head no.

"You were Antigone," I say and she looks at me and smiles.

She sits there for a little bit longer and then a nurse tells her she has to leave. I'm happy Erin comes to see me, but I'm glad she leaves when she does. I feel something rumbling around in my stomach and I think it just might be time to pass some gas.

21

SQUEAKY SHOES

When the doctors say it's okay, I'll get to leave the super-intense intensive care unit and then they're gonna move me to a regular hospital room for a few days and then I get to go home. I can't wait to go home. You know something that's kind of funny? I kind of can't wait to go back to school. I didn't think it was possible. I thought high school was the first-place winner in the category of extreme super-boring things to do, but I guess I was wrong. I mean sitting in a hospital bed is even more boring than school and . . . it's a lot more painful.

So anyway, I'm sitting up in bed playing with some nasty lumpy oatmeal stuff they try to give me for breakfast and my mom is sitting in a corner reading a book, when we hear a knock on the door. We look up and this guy in a suit and tie walks in. He's kind of tall and gangly and all, like he runs marathons or something. He's not wearing one of those hospital badges, and his shoes squeak when he walks across the shiny hospital floor.

"Hi Josh," he says. He looks over at my mom. "Nice to see you again," he says, and then he turns to me and introduces himself. "I'm Detective Jim Fields. I work with the crimes division of the Green Valley Police Department. I want to talk to you about what happened the night you got hurt."

He sits down. I rustle my feet around in the sheets of my bed because all of the sudden I don't feel so great. He starts to ask me questions, lots of questions, who was I with? Did I get in a fight? Did anybody else see the "incident"? I stare at one of the machines that measures my heart. A bright orange line goes up and down real quick like it has the hiccups or something. My mom comes over and sits on the end of my bed. "We need to find out what happened, sweetheart. We have to figure out who did this to you," she says. I keep staring at the heart machine. Finally I look at both of them. "The truth is," I say, "I don't remember," and my head hurts and I feel tired so I ask them to leave me alone.

22

SICK

So they *finally* move me out of the super-intense intensive care unit and move me into a different room in the "regular" part of the hospital. The beds in hospitals are on wheels and stuff, so it's like you're lying down on this huge skateboard with a mattress on it and everything, and when they want to move you they just push your whole bed around with you in it.

So anyway, they give me a new room. I'm like on the third floor or something and I can look out and see the sky and trees and stuff. And I can have visitors too, which is sick. Cody and Niko stop by. They bring me a bunch of skateboard magazines and candy bars. They check out the mummy bandages on my head and then sit in the chairs that are on each side of my bed. We sit there for a while and talk about skateboarding and the sick half-pipe we're gonna build someday. Cody has already drawn up the plans and everything, and we talk about how we're gonna skate when I get out of here, when I start skating again.

I can actually get out of bed and walk around and stuff, but real slow and not too jerky, or my head feels like it's going to explode, so we decide to walk down the hall and back before Cody and Niko have to leave. I shuffle along the hallway in my hospital gown and my tight blue hospital socks. I have boxers on so you can't see my butt flopping around through the openings in these stupid hospital gowns that they make me wear. I know I must look kind of funny—my stupid gown and socks and my head bandaged up so it looks like a giant marshmallow is attached to my neck or something—but Cody and Niko don't say one word about the way I look, or make fun of me or anything.

We walk along the hospital hallway and some of the doors are open to people's rooms and even though you're not supposed to look, sometimes you can't help but see people lying in their hospital beds with all of these machines hooked up to them beeping and buzzing and making weird sounds. There's a lot of sick people in the hospital, but not like "cool" sick, not like "sick air" or "sick ollie" sick, they're just plain old sick. We finish our lap around the hallway and I climb back in bed. I'm pretty tired and Cody and Niko can tell so they leave. I rest my head against the pillow and look out the window before I doze off.

When I open my eyes I see my mom standing in the hallway talking to someone in a quiet voice. I'm not sure who it is at first 'cause my eyes are all blurry and stuff, but when I finally focus I can see that it's that detective guy again. He's wearing a suit and his balled-up fist rests against his hip so that his jacket is kind of swooped back. I can see his gun dangling and his shiny gold badge thingy hanging from his belt. I don't know what they're talking about, but I see him shake his head *no* a few times. My mom looks into my room and sees that I'm awake. She motions to him, and they both walk into my room.

"Detective Fields is here to see you again," she says. I rub my eyes and sit up in my bed a little higher.

"Hi, son," he says, "how you feeling?" They both sit down, and it doesn't take long for Detective Fields to start firing his same old questions at me. "What do you remember from that night? Who were you with? We want to catch these guys. Blah, blah, blah." I look down at my feet, wiggle my toes in the sheets, and give him the same old answer—"I don't know." He stands up and smiles, shakes my hand, tells me he'll be back soon, and turns around and squeaks down the hall.

My mom gets up. She goes to the sink and turns on the faucet. The water slowly gurgles down the drain. She takes one of those white square washcloths, soaks it in the running water, wrings it out, and folds it into a rectangle. She puts it on my forehead and sits on the end of the bed. It feels good . . . cold. "Josh," she says. I look out the window. The sun is setting. I can't wait to go home.

23

YODA

The good news is, my head *will* get better—and it'll get *all* the way better too, eventually. That's what the doctors say anyway. They make me take all these tests and stuff to see if my brain still works and luckily it does. But they say I have to take it slow, real slow. I get headaches and stuff and I get really tired from the smallest things, like walking down the hallway, but each day I can walk a little farther. They say that I'll even be able to skate again, as long as I start out really slow and wear a good helmet. Of course my mom is super freaked-out and concerned. You know, what if I hit my head again—all that worrying mom kind of stuff—but my dad, he's fine with it all. He even says we can use the backyard to build a skate ramp. He told me that that's what he kept whispering in my ear when I was in super-intensive care and stayed asleep for so long. He kept whispering in my ear that I could have a ramp in our backyard if I'd just wake up and my Pops . . . he's a man of his word. Me, Cody, and Niko are gonna build a half-pipe. It's gonna be awesome!

It's getting close to lunchtime, but who cares? The food they serve in the hospital is *totally* heinous, like mystery food, like *what's that you're trying to get me to put in my mouth* food . . . Nasty! Someone comes into my room. I look up. It's Zander, my math tutor, and luckily he's carrying a pizza and a skateboard. He sets down the pizza and gives me a high five. He tells me he's so glad that I'm gonna be okay and that he was super worried when he heard what happened. We sit there and eat pizza and talk and stuff, which I like 'cause usually, when I'm at tutoring, we talk a little bit and then we have to do a bunch of math. But we don't talk about math now, we talk about skating. Zander hands me the board he's carrying and it's brand new and clean and perfect. It has this super-cool logo on the deck and these smooth, neon-blue wheels. It's the most beautiful board I've ever seen. He hands it to me and tells me it's mine.

"It's for when you get out of here and start skating again," he says.

"Sick!"

"This is a state-of-the-art board, the best they make for skating vert ramps."

"Thanks," I say. I lay the deck across my lap and check out the trucks. The metal feels hard and cold in my hand. I reach up and touch the puffy white bandage on my head. Then I look out the window. The tops of trees waver in the wind and the roofs of smaller buildings rest alongside the hospital. It reminds me of standing at the top of the vert ramp. I get this pang in the pit of my stomach and this taste in my mouth like I've been sucking on pennies and all I want to do is get down from there, get my feet on solid ground. I turn to Zander. "Thanks a lot for the board, but I'm not a vert skater," I say.

He opens the pizza box and fishes out a couple more pieces. He hands me a slice and gnaws on a piece of pizza crust. "When you think about it . . . you already are a vert skater," he says.

I tilt my head and look at him like he's lost his marbles.

"Well, think about it . . . You were lying in intensive care *battling* for your life and . . . *you won*. You're a brave cat. It's like you've already dropped into the vert ramp a million times while the whole town was watching . . . *and* . . . you pulled it."

"The vert ramp is *too* sketchy . . . *too* steep," I say.

"But if you decide you want to skate vert, you can do it. What you've been through, Josh . . . you can do anything."

I toss a half-eaten slice into the greasy pizza box and look out the window again. I can't believe that Zander thinks I'm *brave*. I mean, I'd never thought about it like that before—that I had to be *brave* to be in the hospital and stuff. I mean, it just kind of happened to me, that's all.

"Can I tell you something, Zander?" I ask. "And you promise you won't laugh or tell anyone?" He nods his head. "I want to skate vert, I *really* do . . . but when I climb up to the top of those stairs and look down . . . I'm scared. I'm not brave . . . I'm *scared* to do it. Do you know what I mean? And it's not just the vert ramp either . . . other stuff scares me too . . . . About what would happen if I told that detective guy . . . never mind." Zander's quiet and so am I, but he looks at me like he wants me to keep talking. He studies my face for a second, like he can read my mind. He stands up, stares at the horizon, then turns around and looks at me.

"Josh," he says, "skating is like controlled chaos . . . like you take calculated risks, you know what I mean? And sometimes, you just have to go for it . . . you *have* to take the drop even though it's scary. Nothing's gonna happen to you . . . It's gonna be okay. You might feel a little scared, but you have what it takes. You can do it. Trust me . . . I know you can do it. When you're ready, when it feels right . . . you'll know."

"I guess," I say, and I'm not totally sure what he's talking about but I kind of know what he means. That's just Zander. He's a lot like Yoda sometimes.

24

MEN AND MOUSES

Pretty soon, I'll be ready to go home . . . and that's great, 'cause I can't wait for things to get back to normal, so I can skate and go to school and just have my life back. I've been in here for like nine days—okay, so I wasn't awake for like five of them, but still, I feel like I've been here forever. Even though I feel pretty good and all and I can walk around and stuff and they've taken the big, white, mummy bandages off my head, they keep me in here because they say they want to keep an eye on me—make sure there aren't any "complications." Okay, that's cool, but I just want to go home, that's all. The doctors say I should get my rest while I can here in the hospital. Yeah, right! There's somebody in here like twenty-four hours a day, shining a light in my eyes to see if my pupils are moving like they should, or taking my blood pressure, or asking me if I've pooped. You know, if they want you to get rest when you're in the hospital, they should just leave you alone.

I wake up from my nap and when I open my eyes, Erin's sitting in the chair next to my bed reading some book. Erin . . . she's like a total book addict or something. I mean, she doesn't read 'cause she *has* to, like for school and stuff, she reads 'cause she *likes* to. Funny, huh? I woulda never guessed *that* about "the hottest freshman at Valley View High," 'cause in the movies and stuff, they always make the really pretty girls kinda mean or kinda dumb. And Erin . . . she's neither one of those things.

Anyway, my eyes flutter open from my nap and when Erin notices that I'm awake she looks at me and smiles, then she digs around in her backpack for a second and digs out a bunch of cards and pictures and stuff. She tells me that Ms. Moreland had our English class make them for me. We read through them all and they're super nice and some of them are even funny.

Erin asks me if I want to go for a walk down the hallway or something, but there's no way I'm getting out of this bed with her around so she can see me in my boxers and this stupid hospital gown. So we just hang out and talk for a while. We look for something interesting to watch on TV, but there's nothing good on, which is fine with me 'cause I can't watch too much TV or my eyes start to get a little blurry and stuff and my head starts throbbing. We talk about school and things and then finally I ask her something I've been thinking about lately. "Hey, Erin," I say, "have you talked to Brendon?" And she shakes her head no. She hasn't seen him or talked to him since before the night of my "accident." She tells me he never made it to Danny Ramsey's party that night, that she never saw him, and even though he called her a few times since, she hasn't called him back.

Before Erin leaves she digs around in her backpack and fishes out some sort of book-on-CD thing that Ms. Moreland got for me. Ms. M. wants me to listen to it 'cause it's what we're reading in English class right now, and she doesn't want me to be too far behind when I come back to school. It's called *Men and Mouses* or something stupid like that. Perfect—instead of reading a book, I can listen to it, like that's *exactly* how I want to spend my spare time. Erin gathers her things, says good-bye, and leaves.

Pretty soon they bring me a tray with my dinner on it. It's supposed to be turkey, like the kind you get on Thanksgiving. They serve it a lot here, like they want you to celebrate Thanksgiving every single day. But the problem is, the food is so gross I doubt anyone actually eats it. I sure don't. I mean, every stupid thing on my dinner plate is white, except for the soupy cranberries—white turkey meat, white mashed potatoes, whitish, grayish gravy, and vanilla pudding for dessert. I eat the pudding and then push the tray away and wait for them to take it. Lucky for me, my mom and dad show up for the last part of visiting hours. They bring me a sandwich and I eat the whole thing. But pretty soon the nurse comes into my room and tells them visiting hours are over so they have to go home.

So here I am, sitting in my hospital room for another night and I'm totally, 100 percent bored. There's nothing really good on TV and if I look at a magazine for too long I get a headache. I look over and see that book CD thing that Ms. Moreland gave me and there's really nothing for me to do except lie here and stare at the ceiling, so I decide to give it a try. I ring the buzzer and a nurse ducks into my room. "Can you play that book for me?" I say and she picks it up and looks at the title.

"*Of Mice and Men,*" she says, "that's a good one." She leaves the room for a second and comes back with a CD player that she snagged out of the nurses' station. She slides the CD in and pushes PLAY. Some famous guy reads the book and he changes his voice to sound like the characters when they talk. It's actually pretty cool. I turn the lights off in my hospital room and it's all glowy and stuff from all of the hospital equipment and I lie there and listen to some famous guy read to me until I fall asleep.

25

PULL THE TRIGGER

I'm in my hospital room fumbling with the stupid remote control when I hear a knock on the door. It's probably some nurse coming to poke me or check my heart or listen to me breathe or something, but it's not, it's that detective guy, Jim Fields. He's carrying two Styrofoam bowls of something. He hands me one. Chocolate ice cream—stoked! He comes in and asks me how I'm doing and stuff and then he sits in the chair next to my bed. He's not wearing a suit today. He has on a T-shirt with a picture of a guy fishing and some jeans with some running shoes and he's even wearing a ball cap. He actually looks normal. We sit there and eat our ice cream and talk about stuff like skating and fishing. He doesn't ask me anything about "that night," and for a second, I kind of forget I'm talking to a detective. Then I remember the other day when he was standing in the hall talking to my mom. I remember the gun and that shiny gold badge.

"You a cop or a detective?" I ask.

"Well, kind of both," he says.

"So you drive around in a car with lights and sirens and chase criminals and stuff?"

"No lights, no siren," he says and takes a bite of ice cream. "Just an unmarked car."

106

"Like one of those narc guys?"

He laughs a little bit. "Nope, not a narcotics officer either. Narcs go after drugs . . . drug dealers. I'm a detective—I investigate crimes."

"Oh . . . like those CSI guys on TV that pick at dead bodies to find clues and stuff."

"Not exactly . . . you know, it's different . . . different than what you see on TV. Basically I try to solve mysteries, you could say. I try to figure out who did what to who. It's kind of like I have to find all these pieces of a puzzle and then I have to put all the pieces together."

"Pieces of a puzzle?"

"Well, there's the guy, or guys, who committed a crime, right?—that's one piece of the puzzle. Then depending on what happened there's a victim of the crime—that's another piece. And then there's witnesses, that's the next piece. The victim and the witnesses . . . they're important, because they can help me figure out how all of the pieces fit together, and they can testify in court and help put the criminal in jail."

He stands up and puts his hand out toward me. I hand him my empty Styrofoam cup. He tosses it in the trash can next to the door and sits down again. I look out my window. "What happens to the witness piece of the puzzle?" I say, "I mean, if they were there when the crime happens, and they saw it and everything and they just stood there and didn't do anything to stop it, don't they get in trouble too?"

"Nothing happens to the witness."

"Are you sure? I mean if a guy was standing right there and he saw another guy get beat on and stuff and he just stood there staring at his shoes. They don't put a guy like that in jail?"

"Nothing happens to the witness," he says.

Just then a nurse comes in and pushes a couple buttons on some machines. We both watch her fumble around with stuff, and then she leaves the room.

"Hey," I say, "have you ever shot someone before, killed 'em?"

Detective Jim looks at me, and he's quiet for a second. "Yep," he says.

"It's a pretty big deal, huh? . . . I mean taking a guy down and all . . . I don't think I could do it."

"No, you could . . . if you had to, you could. I'm not saying it'd be easy . . . but you could do it."

I stare at the skateboard Zander gave me. It's leaning against the wall in the corner. "Is it scary?" I say.

"Is what scary?"

"You know . . . taking a guy down? . . . I mean like . . . do you feel bad . . . like afterwards and stuff?"

"Well . . . we train for it . . . you know . . . prepare. And then when it happens and you're there and your gun is drawn, there's a lot of adrenaline. You have to know *what* you're doing, but I guess you also have to have it sorted out in your head *why* you're doing it. See . . . you pull the trigger, because you know what you're doing is right . . . The way I look at it—if you have to take one guy down . . . one guy, who's dangerous and could hurt a lot of people . . . you do it . . . you pull the trigger. It's the right thing to do."

I look out the window for a while. Detective Jim puts his elbows on his knees and leans in toward me a little. He looks at his hands and rubs them together. Then he stops and looks me right in the eyes.

"You know, Josh . . . I think you know who did this to you," he says. "But I understand that these things take time. You have to get your head right . . . and I understand that." He reaches into his back pocket, takes out his wallet, and hands me a card with his name and phone number on it and stuff. "You call me anytime you want," he says. He stands up, tells me it's time for him to go, and shakes my hand. "Take care," he says, and I thank him for the ice cream. He turns around and walks away, but this time, his shoes don't squeak when he leaves the room.

LEAVING

The glass doors to the hospital slide open and some nurse dude pushes my wheelchair to the side of the curb. My mom stands next to me, holding a bag of my things. We wait there for like five minutes. I haven't been outside in almost two weeks. Puffy white clouds hang over the foothills in the distance. The sun feels so good on my face and the fresh air—it feels good in my lungs. The family car pulls up to the curb and my dad pops out and opens my door. I get out of the wheelchair and stand there for a second before I climb in. My jeans are baggier than usual and it actually feels kind of good to finally wear shoes. I rub my hand along my buzz-cut hair, gently find the white square bandages that cover the spots where they drilled a couple of holes in my head. I keep my hand there and duck into the backseat of our car.

We drive and after like twenty minutes we pull into our driveway. My mom and dad stand on each side of me and we walk through the front door. My sister comes over and hugs me and my little brother runs up to me and tugs on my arm. I get down on one knee and he hugs me with his whole body. Warm tears slide down my cheeks and I cry. Not because my head hurts or anything. It's just good to be home.

SUCKY ENDINGS

Now that I'm out of the hospital, people can come over to see me whenever they want. One afternoon Erin comes over to hang out. We play some cards and then we just talk. I tell her I listened to that whole book that Ms. Moreland gave me. You know the one, *Of Mice and Men*. I tell her how much I hated the sucky ending 'cause, you know, it's so sad and all. And Erin, she can never say, *Yeah Josh, you're right . . . it sucks . . . school sucks, math sucks,* Antigone *sucks.* Instead she has to say something like, "It *is* sad . . . really sad . . . but I understand why it ended that way." And then of course she has to say something that completely boggles my brain. She says, "Maybe . . . sometimes . . . you have to do something bad, to do something good . . . like in *Of Mice and Men* . . . like, maybe, sometimes . . . you have to be a bad friend to be a good one."

"Whatever," I say. "The ending still sucks!"

Erin grabs her backpack and starts putting stuff in it 'cause she's gotta go home. She's busy grabbing her stuff and I sit there, staring at the ceiling. "Hey, Erin," I say, "can I tell you something?" She stops what she's doing and looks at me. "I remember what happened that night," I say. "I remember who was there and what they did and everything. I remember all of it . . . until I blacked out." And then I tell her the whole story. I tell her about Lenny and

Junior and Brendon. I look at my bedspread and play with a thread that's starting to unravel. She stands up and comes over to me. "What are you going to do?" she says.

"I don't know."

She stands there for a second. "I'll come by and see you tomorrow, okay?" She grabs her backpack, heaves it onto her shoulder, turns around, and leaves.

28

PUZZLE PIECES

I have to go to this physical therapy stuff like every day to get my brain back in shape. But in a couple weeks I'll be done with all that stuff and then I get to go back to school. My mom takes me to my therapy session, then drops me off at home and goes to the grocery store. I'm sitting in my backyard, looking at a skate magazine and enjoying the midmorning sun, when the doorbell rings. I'm the only one home so I cruise over and open the front door. I can't believe my eyes when I see who's standing there. It's Brendon. He stares down at the front step for a second and then mumbles, "Hey, how's it going?"

"Okay," I say and stand there in my sweatpants and socks for a while because I'm not sure what to do. Finally I say, "Do you want to come in?" And he nods and comes inside. We go upstairs to my room. I start to fumble through some video games to look for some of the old ones we used to play.

"I don't really feel like playing," Brendon says. I stop shuffling through the games and stare at the carpet. "Sorry I didn't come and see you in the hospital," he says, ". . . I hate hospitals." I keep staring at the carpet. I don't say anything and neither does he and then I look at him.

"Why didn't you do something?" I say.

"What are you talking about?"

"You *know* what I'm talking about . . . *That* night . . . the night they hit me."

"Josh, don't . . . let's not do this . . . maybe I should—"

"You saw what they did. They could've killed me. They could—"

"I didn't see it. I didn't see any of it."

"You were standing right there. You saw Junior grab me, you saw Lenny hit me, and you didn't do anything . . . nothing—you just stood there."

"I—"

"It wasn't cool what they did . . . they're not good for you . . . they're not good for anybody . . . they need to pay."

"Well, whaddya gonna do? Rat 'em out?"

"It's a stupid rule, don't you think?"

"Who said anything about rules? It's not a *rule,* it's just something you don't do. You don't *rat* people out. It's not cool."

"Dude . . . they almost *killed* me! Do you get that? They almost *killed* me—I could have died!" I look down at my feet. My face feels red and hot and stuff and my heart pounds in my head. Finally I look up. "I need you to be a witness," I say, and Brendon just stands there staring out my bedroom window.

I look up and see the skate poster on my wall—the one where Danny Way is flying over the wall of China. I've stared at that poster a million times, and I never really noticed that even though there's a bunch of people down on the ground watching him shoot across the sky like some kind of crazy comet, his one arm stretched out like a bird, the other hand clutching his board keeping it stuck to his feet so he can make the landing . . . even though there's people everywhere watching him blaze through the sky, when he's skating, he's alone . . . totally alone. Finally Brendon looks at me. "I already told you . . . I didn't see anything." Then he turns around and walks out of my room. I hear him clomp down the stairs taking them two at a time. The front door slams shut and he's gone.

I sit in my room for a while, sit at my desk, and thumb through an old skate magazine. I open one of the desk drawers and see that book on CD that Ms. Moreland gave me. I think about that famous guy's voice and the way that story had such a sad ending and I remember what Erin said, that thing about being a bad friend to be a good one, and I think for once I might understand what she means. I fumble through the drawer, fumble through all of the different cards and stuff that people sent me while I was in the hospital until I find what I'm looking for. I rub Detective Jim Fields's business card between my fingers. I go downstairs, pick up the phone, and dial.

LOST IN THE WILDERNESS

Detective Jim Fields comes over and him and me and my parents sit in my living room. I tell them everything I remember—I tell them about Lenny and Junior and stupid Brendon standing there looking at his shoes. My mom cries the whole time, especially when I get to the part where Lenny hits me with the skateboard and my dad sits there sighing and shaking his head. Detective Jim writes down everything I say and he tells me that he's taking my "official statement."

When I'm done we all walk over to the front door. Detective Jim shakes my hand and tells me that I'm doing the right thing . . . that he's proud of me. After he leaves I ask my mom and dad what's going to happen now that I've spilled the beans. My mom tells me there's probably going to be a trial in a few months and I'm going to have to testify. She says I'm going to have to wear a suit and tie and maybe even some shoes that squeak. And I'm fine with all of it, I mean I'll do it, I'll testify, I'm just not sure about the shoes, that's all.

I start back to school a couple weeks later. At first I'm kind of scared. I mean, I'm not sure what people are going to think about me telling on Lenny. You know, no one likes a rat and all, but people . . . they're super cool to me. People I don't even know come up to me and welcome me back. Danny Ramsey even comes up to me at lunch and shakes my hand. The king of the jocks shakes my hand. I can't believe it.

Erin comes over to my house all the time to study and just hang out. My parents treat her like she's a rock star or something. Turns out my mom and dad met her for the first time in the emergency room the night I got hit. Someone from Danny Ramsey's party gave Erin a ride over to the hospital and she sat there and waited around with my mom and dad for a long time. She stayed there until her parents came and got her and they practically had to drag her out of that place 'cause she didn't want to leave. I guess she would've sat there all night if her parents let her, but she was tired and upset, so they made her go home. Now my parents think she's like a goddess or something. The funny thing is—I never thought a girl could be my best friend. I mean I know I'm probably never gonna skate with Erin and all. But I have Cody and Niko and other people to do that with. It's okay that she's not a skater, she's still a totally cool friend.

Cody and Niko and my dad and me are building a super-sick half-pipe in our backyard. It'll be done in a couple more weeks and Zander's gonna come over and skate it with us. But the really good news is Lenny can't come near me. The police arrested him, put him in jail, and his mom wouldn't pay the money to get him out on bail. Now he's locked up until we have the trial. I haven't seen Brendon since he came by my house that day. I think he's at Sunrise Continuation, but I'm not really sure. I asked Cody and Niko, and they say he hasn't been at the skate park either. I guess he's just floating around out there, lost in the wilderness. The truth is, I kind of feel sorry for him. I'm not mad at him anymore, I just kind of feel sorry for him, that's all.

I guess sometimes the hardest part about being a friend is that there's not too much you can do really when your friend's lost in the wilderness. I mean you can try to help him not get lost in the first place. You can reach out your hand and tell him come this way, don't go over there—it's steep and gnarly and treacherous. But there's not a whole lot you can do if he won't reach out his hand and grab back. And I think that's the hardest part about friendship—standing by and watching your friend wander into the forest where it's cold and dark and lonely and knowing there's not one thing you can do.

30

PREPARING FOR BATTLE

The doctors say my brain is totally better. All the swelling's gone down and it's exactly the size it's supposed to be. Not too big, not too small . . . just right, and that's the best thing ever 'cause the doctors say I can skate again. My mom's super freaked out so my dad has to keep reminding her that in the three years I've been skating, I've never hit my head once. "He knows what he's doing, he knows how to fall," he keeps telling her. And it's true, I do know how to fall, so now there's only one thing left to do . . . prepare for battle.

Cody, Niko, and me meet at the skate park like practically every afternoon. The first day back on my skateboard, my legs are kind of wobbly and stuff. I take it easy over in mini land and skate with the young kids. I drop in on the little three-foot quarter-pipes. The board Zander gave me is super sick. The wheels are all smooth and glidy and it feels like you're floating on air.

I spend days just riding small bank ramps and mini quarter-pipes dropping in and carving turns. It feels so good to be skating again. I go and hang out with Cody and Niko over at the mini half-pipe and watch them do airs and grind the super-buttery coping. After a few days of epic sessions in mini land, Cody and Niko talk me into dropping in on the small half-pipe, which is only about five feet high, but still kind of sketchy if you haven't done it in a while.

I stand on the deck of the small half-pipe, look down, and I know I'm ready. I don't feel scared or anything even though I haven't dropped in on anything this steep in like four months. I set my back wheels against the coping then stomp on the front of my board and swoosh into the ramp just like that. Cody and Niko give me high fives and slap me on the shoulder and tell me I'm ripping. It's almost time to leave but before we go we decide to climb up to the top of the vert ramp. We race up the two flights of stairs, lean our boards against the railing, and peer down into the belly of the beast.

"Dude, it's *so* steep!" Niko says.

"Frickin' impossible," Cody mutters, and we stand there at the top of the ramp looking down its steep, totally vert walls for a while. The sun starts to dip slowly behind the foothills, and all the skaters who are left in the skate park head for the gate.

"I guess you just have to be ready," I say and we turn around, grab our boards, and leave.

31

SLAYING THE BEAST

Cody, Niko, and me start this thing where after we're done skating the mini half-pipe, we go over to the vert ramp. We start at the very bottom and start pumping the walls. Just the other day, I started from the bottom and made it like fifteen feet up the side of the ramp, all the way to the coping. It was *so* sick! Today we do the usual—meet at the skate park after school, pay our three dollars, put on our stinky pads, and skate, but this afternoon Cody and Niko have to leave early.

I go over to the street course. I think maybe Brendon will be there, but he's not. I look around and for some reason things look different, like they changed the layout of the street course around a little bit or something. I mean, it still has the same stuff and all—stairs, funboxes, gaps, rails—it just looks different to me, that's all. There's a few skaters messing around, busting kickflips onto boxes and tail sliding along the edges, but I don't feel like skating any of the street course stuff. I head over to the vert ramp and no one's on it. The grandpas are busy skating the pool and a few kids are messing around in mini land, but the vert ramp is totally empty.

I walk over, stand at the bottom of the beast, and look up its towering walls. I stand there for a while, spinning the wheels on the board that Zander gave me. My wheels are all warm and smooth and worn in perfect and they make this cool swooshing sound as they spin around on the trucks. I look at my watch—fifteen minutes before the park closes. Skaters start to peel off their sweaty pads and head toward the gate.

I turn around and start to leave, but for some reason I stop and look at the beast one more time and before I know it, I'm climbing to the top of the stairs. It's so high up there you can see everything in the distance. If you really focus and look way beyond the trees, you can even kind of see my house. I stand up there alone and look around a while, then I grab my board and set it down on the deck of the ramp. I plant one foot on the tail and look down into the belly of the beast. My heart races. I take a deep breath and stand there for a long time. And it's just like Zander said it would be, I'm kind of scared, but it feels right and I know that I'm ready.

I stomp down on the front of my board and drop in. I lean forward, press my shoulders into my feet, lean into the face of it. I race down the wall and I'm going fast, super fast, but my wheels dig in, grab the surface, super smooth, super buttery. I get to the bottom of the ramp, bend my knees—my board's glued to my feet underneath me solid—and I fly, shoot up the other side. I see coping, pop the tail, reach down, grab my board with one hand, and I am flying, soaring above it all—Valley View High . . . Old Oaks Park . . . Lenny, Brendon . . . Zander, Niko and Cody . . . Mom, Dad, and Erin—it's all down there, glued to the earth's surface, and I'm floating, weightless. I am Danny Way, flying through the air, launching over the wall of China, one arm stretched out like the wing of a bird, the other clutching the board to my feet so I can make the landing. I am Josh Lowman, skating vert, slaying the beast, floating, flying, soaring above it all, and I am free.

QUESTIONS FOR DISCUSSION

1. Compare the behavior of skaters at Green Valley skatepark to the behavior of skaters at Old Oaks Park. How does having rules or not having rules influence the way people behave?

2. Would you rather skate at Old Oaks Park, Green Valley skatepark or street skate? Why?

3. On pages 33-34 Josh's mother complains about the way skaters act at Old Oaks park. How does Josh's opinion of the skaters at Old Oaks Park differ from his mother's? Who do you agree with and why?

4. Josh is beginning to believe the stereotype that all skaters are "dirt-bags," but on page 66, Josh and his math tutor Zander talk about the different kinds of people who skate. How does Zander help Josh think about skaters in a new way?

5. When Josh and Erin are talking about the novel, *Of Mice and Men*, Erin tells Josh, "Maybe . . . sometimes. . .you have to do something bad, to do something good . . .like maybe sometimes . . .you have to be a bad friend to be a good one." What do you think Erin means here? Do you agree or disagree with what she says about friendship? Why?

6. There is a pivotal scene toward the end of *Vertical* in which Josh stares at a poster of Danny Way airing over the wall of China. Josh points out that ". . . even though there's people everywhere watching (Danny Way) blaze through the sky, when (Danny Way's) skating, he's alone . . ." What impact does this realization have on Josh?

7. What does Josh learn about Erin as he gets to know her better and what kind of influence does their friendship have on Josh?

8. When Josh and Erin are talking about the play *Antigone* Erin says, ". . . maybe sometimes you have to make up your own rules, do what you think is right, then no matter what, you win, no matter what other people say." Explain what you think she means here. Do you agree or disagree with this idea? Why?

9. What does Josh learn about dropping in on the vert ramp and what does he learn about falling? What lessons do skaters learn from skateboarding that they can apply to other areas of their lives?

10. On page 52, Josh explains that Antigone goes against her uncle's rigid rules to stand up for something that she knows is right. On pages 92-3, Josh tells Erin that the night Erin saved his life, she acted like Antigone. Explain what you think Josh means here.

11. One of the unspoken rules that Josh believes he must follow is "no body likes a rat". Does this unspoken rule exist in your community? When is it okay to break this rule?

12. Josh goes along with the idea that "no one likes a rat" even though he knows that Lenny is doing bad things in his community. What would have happened if Josh had never told the truth about Lenny to Detective Jim Fields? What would have happened if he had told the authorities about Lenny sooner when Lenny stole credit cards from Mrs. Thompson?

13. Do you think skaters should wear helmets? Why or why not?

14. Why does Josh keep referring to school as a prison? How does his attitude toward school change by the end of the novel?

15. Josh Lowman loves skating and he is committed to skating whenever he can. What do you love to do? How does having an activity that you're passionate about affect your life?

GLOSSARY OF SKATEBOARDING TERMS

Air—riding off a ramp or jump and boosting into the air. Examples: He shot out of the ramp and got huge **air**.

Bank Ramp—a ramp shaped like a triangle with a sloped surface

Coping—a round, raised lip, usually made out of pipe, that is attached to the top edge of skateboard ramps and along the edges of bowls.

Gaps—spaces between two surfaces that skaters air or jump over. The skater skates along one surface, launches over a gap and then lands on the other side of the gap on the second surface.

Grind—riding or scraping along an edge, such as coping, a rail, curb or bench, using the trucks of the skateboard instead of the wheels.

Grind Rails—rails made for skateboarders to grind on.

Half Pipe—a ramp shaped like the bottom half of a pipe that has been cut in half horizontally.

Indy—while in the air, the skater reaches his/her back hand down and grabs the middle of the board, between the feet, on the side of the board where his/her toes are pointing

Kick Flip—the skateboarder pops the board into the air, then flicks the board with his/her front foot. The board spins underneath the skater once, before he/she catches the board, deck side up with his/her feet and lands wheels down continuing to skate. Note: the board doesn't rotate underneath the skater horizontally, like the blade of a helicopter, but spins like a hotdog on one of those roller grill things at convenience stores.

Mini ramp—usually a small version of a half pipe. Mini ramps are usually shorter than the rider and there is no vertical drop.

Nollie—the skateboarder slaps the nose of the skateboard against the pavement and pops the board into the air keeping his/her feet on the deck of the board while flying through the air. A nollie is an ollie, but the skater gets his/her board into the air by using the nose of the skateboard instead of using the tail.

Nollie Big Spin—the skateboarder nollies, shoving the skateboard with his/her foot so that the board rotates 360 degrees, like the blade of a helicopter underneath him/her *and* rotates his/her body 180 degrees backside all at the same time. Because the rider has roated his/her body 180 degrees while in the air, when he/she lands, the back foot is now at the nose of the board and the front foot is at the tail of the board.

Ollie—while riding along, the skateboarder pops the tail of the skateboard against the ground, jumps up and slides his/her front foot forward against the deck of the board. The skateboard is propelled into the air and floats directly underneath the skater.

Rock to Fakie—the skateboarder pops the nose of the skateboard over the coping, rocks onto the underside of the board for a split second, pops the trucks back over the lip and rolls back down the ramp.

Tailslide—sliding along an edge, such as coping, a rail, curb or bench, using the underside of the tail end of the board, instead of the wheels.

Trucks—the front and rear axle assemblies that are mounted to the underside of the skateboard, connecting the wheels to the deck of the board and allowing the rider to turn.

Vert Ramp—a giant half pipe ramp, usually at least 12 feet tall, with steep vertical sides at the top. A vert ramp is kind of shaped like the letter "U".

50-50—the skateboarder grinds along an edge, such as coping, a rail, curb or bench, with weight distributed equally on both the trucks of the skateboard instead of the wheels.

Photo by Trish Portella-Wright

Janet Eoff Berend loves to swim, surf, play music, read, cook, and write. She teaches English at La Costa Canyon High School and enjoys life with her husband, two kids, and dog in Encinitas, California. She doesn't drop in on vert ramps, but deeply admires those who do.